MW01042441

Rock Lake Station
Settlement Stories Since 1896

By Gaye I. Clemson

With Major Contributions from Robert Taylor and William Greer

Note for Librarians: A cataloguing record for this book is available from Library and Archives Canada at www.collectionscanada.ca/amicus/index-e.html
ISBN 1-4120-6626-3

Cover Design and Layout by Troy Chasey/Capitola Design, Santa Cruz, CA.

Photographs made available through the family collections of Robert Taylor and William Greer assembled over many generations.

Printed in Victoria, BC, Canada. Printed on paper with minimum 30% recycled fibre. Trafford's print shop runs on "green energy" from solar, wind and other environmentally-friendly power sources.

PUBLISHING

Offices in Canada, USA, Ireland and UK

This book was published *on-demand* in cooperation with Trafford Publishing. On-demand publishing is a unique process and service of making a book available for retail sale to the public taking advantage of on-demand manufacturing and Internet marketing. On-demand publishing includes promotions, retail sales, manufacturing, order fulfilment, accounting and collecting royalties on behalf of the author.

Book sales for North America and international:
Trafford Publishing, 6E–2333 Government St.,
Victoria, BC v8т 4р4 CANADA
phone 250 383 6864 (toll-free 1 888 232 4444)
fax 250 383 6804; email to orders@trafford.com
Book sales in Europe:
Trafford Publishing (uk) Limited, 9 Park End Street, 2nd Floor
Oxford, UK oxı ıнн UNITED KINGDOM
phone 44 (0)1865 722 113 (local rate 0845 230 9601)
facsimile 44 (0)1865 722 868; info.uk@trafford.com
Order online at:
trafford.com/05-1537

10 9 8 7 6 5 4 3 2

Dedication and Acknowledgements

This is the third in a series of narratives concerning the human history of Algonquin Park from the perspective of leasehold residents, who have occupied small corners of the park since the earliest days of the 20th century. My first experience of the park was the summer of 1954 when, as a nine-month old, I watched my parents build our little cabin from the safe venue of a bushel basket under a nearby 100+ foot pine tree. Since then I have spent some part of virtually every summer on the shores of Canoe Lake.

My journey of discovery began in 1996 when I first set out in my green cedar strip canoe with my twin two-year old boys to meet and record the settlement stories of some of my Canoe Lake neighbours. After that first venture I was hooked and my efforts took on a life of their own. Many hours have been spent over the last nine years visiting residents from across the depth and breadth of the Park. My collection of stories of their Algonquin Park experiences is now massive and I hope that readers will enjoy this attempt to share another aspect of the human heritage of Algonquin Park.

I can't thank enough Robert Taylor and his wife Mary for their kindness and effort in helping me with a putting the pieces together for this narrative about Rock Lake Station. As a descendent of one of the first full-time residents and a fabulous story teller Robert's wealth of knowledge and insight has been most appreciated. Thanks must also be extended to Joan Barclay Drummond whose recollections and photos of her parents and grandparents Rock Lake experiences were invaluable in helping piece together the areas early history. Another special thanks must also be extended to William Greer for sharing both his knowledge and his photo collection. In addition a note of appreciation to all of the Rock, Galeairy and Whitefish Lake residents who shared their memories including Art Eady, Brian, Helen and Brad Steinberg, Judy Jeffery Hagerman, Rose Campbell, Mary Eleanor Riddell Morris, Peggy Sharpe, Robert Holmes, Leslie and Fred Allan Jr., Helen Beaton, Ruth Welham Umphrey, Mary Fretz and Robert Miller. Last but not least, many thanks must go to fellow Algonquin Park historian Rory MacKay, Ron Tozer, retired Park Naturalist, and my dear Aunt June Noninski who have all provided me with great support with the proofing and editing of this narrative.

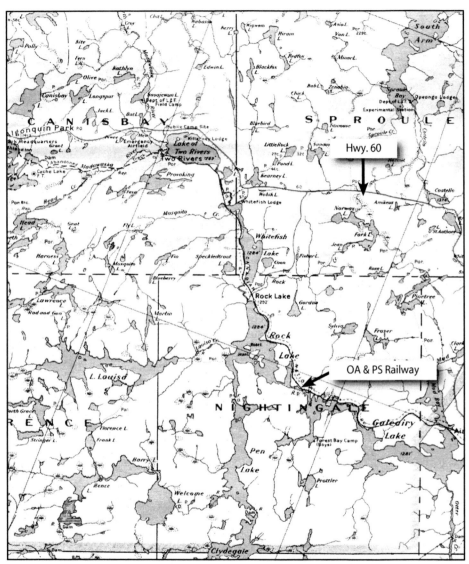

Rock Lake Station Area 1956 Province of Ontario Map No. 47a Department of Lands and Forests, Surveys and Engineering Division

Prologue

Rob Taylor has invited me to attend the Rock Lake/Whitefish Lake Residents' Association annual meeting and suggests that if I come a few hours early he'd be willing to take me on a guided tour of the two lakes. It's a bit embarrassing, for even though I am a 50-year resident of Algonquin Park I have never ventured forth into either Rock or Whitefish lakes and have no sense of the community that resides there whatsoever. But what better way is there to improve my knowledge than to be given a personal tour by one of their finest storytellers?

Rock Lake is located on the east side of the Park, at kilometer marker 40.3, and is well known today as the location of one of the main public campgrounds in the Park. It is however quite a way south of the highway; eight kilometers to be exact. The winding dirt road runs parallel to a beautiful rock face. I reach the campground and make my way past the Park Office and the river landing. Bearing to the right I wend my way down a narrow track, complete with potholes, roots and rocks that are ready to do major damage to my car's undercarriage. At the third entry road on the right, I soon find a sign (green letters painted on an old oar) directing me to the Taylor cottage that was built around 1950 by Dr. Alexander Dunn, a dentist from Orillia. In 1992 his daughter Doreen decided to sell, which is how the Taylors were able to return to Algonquin Park. My own cabin is water access only, so it takes me a few minutes to adjust to the idea of being able to 'drive' in to the cottage.

Robert and his wife Mary hear the sounds of my car and come out to greet me. Mary has a ready smile and a sweetness that is captivating and delightful. I hope that I'll be able at some point to get to know her better. Robert, who tells me to call him Rob, is a giant bear of a man with a shock of white hair and a jolly look about him somewhat reminiscent of old European photographs of St. Nick. There is however about both of them an aura of sadness. I find out later that their 25 year-old daughter Natasha had died in 1999 after a long illness. As a neighbour Helen Steinberg later told me:

> *"Natasha had a consuming love for her beloved Algonquin, and delighted in being here. She had a quiet strength of character and a determination to live life to the fullest in spite of her illness. She had a unique and distinctive tone to her voice, and on quiet summer evenings, her joyous laughter would often echo over the tree tops to our place."*[1]

The Taylor's cabin sits right along the Madawaska River, which flows about 10-12 boat lengths wide right outside the front door. This means that travelers upon the river pass within feet of the Taylor's dock. The noise of a powerboat halts our conversation as it races past at a speed too fast for the river. It's wake causes the small Taylor boat tied up at the dock to shake madly, tugging fiercely at the bow and stern painters whose double knots hold it securely to the dock. It occurs to me that those water currents must play havoc on the stability of both the shoreline, the dock cribs, the dock rings as well as the painters.

Before we venture out onto the lake, Rob has decided that we need to first investigate Rock Lake Station. I look at him with a blank look on my face – which he takes to be an open invitation to begin his tale. I take out my notebook and begin to write furiously as we back track down the dirt track and park the car next to the Rock Lake Campground Office. As I look around me all I see is a shower/washroom complex to my right, a hill to my left, a long and very straight paved road ahead and nearby an open field covered with a mix of grass and scrub bushes that blocks the path down to the lake. Rob begins his narrative.

It turns out that over a hundred years ago there used to be a railway line that ran right through here. In fact, I am standing on what was once the main line. This explains why the road ahead is so straight, as the main entrance

---

[1] Recollections from Rock Lake resident Helen Steinberg 2004.

road to the campground goes right down the rail bed for most of its length. Rob's grandfather, William J. McCourt, was one of the first residents of Rock Lake way back in 1896. John Rudolphus Booth, the noted lumberman, had hired him to help manage a gravel pit whose contents were used to fill the rail beds. Later, once the railroad was completed, McCourt stayed on and became the first Rock Lake station agent and dispatcher, working out of a little hut located right next to the track, just south of Rock Creek.

Rob stomps around waving his hands emphatically. For a few minutes I am concerned that the Park officials are going to think us insane and call for the OPP to cart us away to the closest medical centre for observation. But gradually I begin to see what Rob can see. The remains of the foundations for various buildings including his family home start to emerge in my imagination out of the grass and shrubs. To my left I see the lilac and rose bushes now fiercely overgrown, and when looking carefully can see the remains of his grandmother's telephone box imbedded in the bushes and the edges of what must have been a back garden. He describes to me in great detail and shows me the locations of Rock Lake Station No. 1 & No. 2, the water tower, the pump house and Gulland water stand, Charlie Burns cabin, the Rock Lake grocery store, the boathouse, Aunt Eva's cabin, the double section house and the old rangers shelter hut. Farther down the road, at Rock Lake Campsite No. 2, he shows me the location of the Baulke cottages at Baulke's Point where many a Rock Lake leasehold family first experienced and grew to love Algonquin Park. According to Rob, at one time there was even a Rock Lake school (S.S. #1 Nightingale) that was part of the Haliburton School Board.

We retrace our steps to the Taylor cottage, jump into the boat and head south down the river towards Rock Lake. Just past the landing, Rob points out Rock Creek where one of the local residents in the 1940s decided that he wanted a deeper channel. He brought in some explosives and blasted himself a little harbour, to the absolute horror of the local Park Ranger. Out in the lake the beautiful beach, which is now part of the campground, becomes clearly visible, but what is more vivid is the old rail bed that runs straight as a die along the east shore of the lake, several feet above the water line in spots. The rail bed is overgrown now with shrubs and small spruce trees covering most of its length. As we get closer to the eastern shore, out of the morning mist appears this huge rock and cement edifice that stands at least four feet high off of the water. It apparently is the remains of a three-slip two-story boathouse that once graced the shore. It's part of what was originally the Fleck and later the Barclay Estate. Andrew W. Fleck was an engineer, a key J. R. Booth business associate, Secretary Treasurer of the Ottawa Arnprior and Parry Sound Railway and later a Booth son-in-law due to his marriage to Booth's only surviving daughter, Helen Gertrude Booth.

We tie up the boat and walk around land that is now overgrown with 30 foot high scrub spruce on what I am told was originally the front lawn. Further back we can see traces of the foundations of what must have been a massive house. A short half-a-mile bushwhack in the woods brings us to the remains of a tennis court on which net postholes and pavement markers are still visible. In the middle of the surface is a huge hole full of small pebbles. It was the site of a huge fire that the Ministry of Natural Resources, then called, Department of Lands and Forests set to burn leftover debris after the estate buildings had been burned in 1956. Rob tells me that nearby are the remains of a stable, the family's private railway siding, and a train station. All I can see is bush, so I need to use my imagination to speculate on what must have once been here over 50 years ago.

Returning to the boat we do a quick tour of the rest of the lake, as time is running short. We motor past a big high bluff called Cathedral Rock by some and Perley Rock by others, from which the ashes of many a resident's loved one have been thrown. It's named after W. G. Perley an Ottawa lumberman and partner of J.R. Booth in building the Canadian Atlantic Railway that connected Ottawa with Boston and opened in 1882. Rob reminisces that, when he was a young whippersnapper, one of the adventures for all of the youth of the lake was to jump off a ledge part way up the rock face. I am horrified as I immediately picture my twin sons doing just that.

As we head back up the lake we motorpast the two islands Jean and Rose, named after Fleck's two daughters. Nearby the high rock face called Booth's Rock, and called by some as Booth's nose, named after J. R. Booth, dominates the horizon. Rob tells me that there is now a hiking trail that winds its way up to a lookout site at the top. I make myself a mental note that next summer I should take my twin boys on The Booth Rock Trail hike to see the view. He goes on to say that in 1996 a forest fire destroyed all of the trees on the ridge for several acres. Luckily Rock Lake leaseholders saw the smoke, were the first to notify the park officials, and rushed to start a bucket brigade to fight it in its earliest stage.

Next we go past Chamberlain Rock, another massive rock bluff, that apparently one can crawl up inside if one is wiry and skinny enough. Local armchair geologists suspect that at one time it might have been connected to Perley Rock. It must have also had some spiritual significance, as near the water line, barely visible, are the red ochre markings of native Indian pictographs. Not recognizable now, Rob comments that to him the images looked like a slain deer stretched out and some curved lines.

Once again we retrace our steps, but this time we head north up the Madawaska River, under the iron railway bridge and head out into Whitefish Lake. Rob continues his narrative with the soft drone of the boat engine in the background. Whitefish Lake is today a shadow of its former self. There are only a few cottages left dotting the landscape here and there, mostly at the south end. The rest are long gone, noticeable only because the forest hasn't yet reclaimed the land upon which they sat.

Instead of heading straight to the meeting place, Rob takes a small detour to show me Tillie's pasture, where his Aunt Tillie lived in a tarpaper shack at the turn of the century. Just north across the lake a little way are the remains of what was once a tourist fishing camp called Whitefish Lodge. Just south are the remains of what was Camp Douglas a boy's camp that had a short life on the lake in the 1950s. We turn around and head to the meeting where the local residents warmly welcome me. As I gaze at the crowd, I wonder what other tales lie beneath the surface of their smiling faces. I am determined to find out.

Chamberlain Rock Today

Pearley Rock Today

Rock Lake Log Boom and Aligator c 1930's

Rock Lake View looking south from a hill overlooking the station c 1910

Looking towards Baulke Point from Rock Lake Station c 1920s

Vernon McCourt (L) and cousin Eddie Richardson (R) c 1920

The Railway Beginnings

I t all began for the little community at Rock Lake in 1896, when John Rudolphus Booth, a well-known lumberman from Ottawa who at 'one time had some of the largest timber and sawmill interests in the empire', decided to build a railway from Parry Sound to Ottawa.[2] He wanted access to the shipping of wheat and other products from western Canada and the mid-western United States to Ottawa, Montreal and points south into the United States. Though primarily a lumberman, Booth's interest in railroads had started in the early 1880s when he had financed the building of a rail line, which ran from Ottawa to Boston.[3] According to Rory MacKay, an Algonquin Park historian and resident of nearby Lake of Two Rivers:

> "Ottawa provided too small a market for the [Canadian Atlantic Railway], so in 1892 Booth began the Ottawa, Arnprior and Parry Sound line, which crossed the Ottawa-Huron Tract through Booth's timber limits. The line followed the Bonnechère Valley to Golden Lake, crossed to the Madawaska Valley and [passed through the southern end of Algonquin Park]. From there it went on to Georgian Bay at Depot Harbour, just south of Parry Sound. The total distance was [just under 400 miles]."[4]

By early 1896 thirty camps had been built along the newly surveyed right-of-way that could accommodate up to 2,000 workers. Six hundred men

---

[2] *Algonquin,* by Rory MacKay and William Reynolds pg. 43.
[3] *J. R. Booth Life and Times of an Ottawa Lumber King,* by John Ross Trinnell pg. 109.
[4] *Algonquin,* by Rory MacKay and William Reynolds, pgs. 43/44.

with 150 teams were busy on construction with 50 new men being hired every day. Special trains delivered 150 tons of dynamite from the Ottawa Powder Works of Buckingham, Quebec that was needed to blast the line through the Precambrian rock along the route. The dynamite was stored in magazines built on islands on nearby lakes.[5] In the process of laying out the right-of-way, the surveyors came upon a natural glacial sand and gravel deposit that lies between Whitefish and Rock Lakes (two lakes, which at the time lay south of the Algonquin Park boundary). This sand and gravel was perfect as ballast for the railway bed, so J. R. Booth hired William John McCourt, son of a great lakes sea captain named Captain William Haney McCourt, to manage the gravel pits during the railway construction.

For unknown reasons Captain William's namesake, William John, known to all as Billie, had no interest in the sea captain's life, and had trained to be a telegrapher. So in the fall of 1896 when one of the railway's main contractors, D. C. MacDonald, announced to Booth that he'd 'have the rails laid between Whitney and Cache Lake by August, to the Gilmour Mills at Canoe Lake by mid-September, and the line finished in an additional two months', Billie decided to stay on. Quickly he was appointed to be the station agent at the newly named Rock Lake Station.[6] The first Rock Lake 'day station', with the Morse code call letters "UF", was built just south of the Rock Creek Bridge at milepost 156.1 from Ottawa. It was an instrumented boxcar located on a siding near Rock Lake, with living accommodation at the other end of the car.

In mid-November the line was officially opened for freight business by Andrew W. Fleck, who was the secretary-treasurer for the line. To celebrate, Booth hosted a special run from Ottawa to Potter's Lake (80 miles east of Parry Sound). He invited 100 passengers including members of parliament, senators and newspapermen, feeding them lunch on the way up and dinner on the way back. Attached to the rear of the train, was Booth's recently completed official business railcar No. 99, which he called 'Opeongo'[7]. It was on this trip that he earned the moniker 'King of Canadian Lumbermen

[5] *J. R. Booth Life and Times of an Ottawa Lumber King*, by John Ross Trinnell pgs. 31/32.
[6] *J. R. Booth Life and Times of an Ottawa Lumber King*, by John Ross Trinnell pg.48.
[7] Likely named after nearby Lake Opeongo, which means 'Sandy at the Narrows' where it is believed, there was at one time an Indian settlement. According to Algonquin Park Bulletin No. 10 – *Names of Algonquin* there was also a colonization road projected from near Renfrew towards Opeongo Lake that in 1850 was called the Opeongo Road.

and Railway's from W.C. Edwards, a Member of Parliament at the time.[8] On December 5, 1896 the then Prime Minister, Wilfred Laurier, and Booth went on an inspection tour of the line that then opened for passenger traffic on December 21, 1896. At the time, return fare from Ottawa to Parry Sound was $14.85, with a special Christmas excursion fare that year of $5.50 to celebrate the Christmas season.[9]

The first regularly scheduled trains from the Ottawa, Arnprior and Parry Sound Railway (OA&PS) rolled through the newly minted Rock Lake Station on the new rails in January 1897.[10] In 1898, letters patent for right-of-way and station-grounds were finally officially granted to the railway for nearly 30 acres in the vicinity of the station. The station location was ideal due to its close proximity to Rock Creek, where water flowing from Fisher Lake provided an ample supply for the thirsty steam locomotives. However, to get the water from the creek to the water tower was no easy matter. A huge ten-inch diameter pipe came down through the center of the water tower, and fed a two-inch Gulland type water standpipe that stood between the two tracks. It was able to fill the steam engines of trains going in either direction. The huge water tower had to be fed continuously with a steam pump located in a nearby small pump house that was used to draw water from the creek.[11] A fellow named Charlie Burns was hired for 50 cents a day to man the steam pump and fill the steam locomotive engines seven days a week. Later, after the Rock lake area became part of Algonquin Park, Charlie built himself a small cabin that caused much consternation with local park officials, since it was erected without permission from either them or the railway. Though Charlie's cabin is long gone, as late as 1945 the remains of Charlie's two-holer outhouse could be seen at the second bend in the creek where an old wooden wagon trail bridge crossed the creek. The standpipe foundation can still be seen by an observant railway enthusiast under what is now the Rock Lake Campground access road. An identical Gulland standpipe system was also used at Algonquin Park Station on Cashe Lake to provide water for the steam trains passing through there in this same way.

The first OA&PS railway foreman at Rock Lake Station was John Froebel.

[8.] *J. R. Booth Life and Times of an Ottawa Lumber King,* by John Ross Trinnell pgs. 51-53.

[9.] *J. R. Booth Life and Times of an Ottawa Lumber King,* by John Ross Trinnell pg. 61.

[10.] The original Rock Lake Station sign still exists and is mounted at a cottage on Rock Lake.

[11.] A picture of the water tank can be found in the Algonquin Park Visitor Centre and to this date, if one looks closely, one can still see the concrete feet of this monster tank at the head of the Rock Lake Campsite No. 1.

Soon after William McCourt's arrival, Frobel decided to build a one-room tarpaper shack for his new wife Ottelie Emile Neuman, whom he had married in 1895. It was located on the south shore of the top end of Whitefish Lake, just east of the newly laid railway bed. According to Robert (McCourt) Taylor, the Neuman family had come to Canada in 1884. The 'Baron', as he was known had been an official in the German Government in the 1850s, but was disgraced when he married below his rank to a woman he loved. He lost his government position and became a brick manufacturer with a facility located on the German/Dutch border. For unknown reasons he abandoned this business, came to Canada, and settled at Waito Station (a small station located west of Pembroke). They had two daughters, Ottelie (born in 1871 and known as Tillie) and Ida (born in 1881). John and Tillie moved to the Whitefish Lake shack, which did have running water and coal oil lamps for light. Fellow railway workers would throw scoops of coal off the tenders as they went past, providing the Froebel's with plenty of heat in the winter. John would shovel the coal into a large bin beside the shack for easy winter access. Many years later one of the steam train locomotives derailed east of nearby Men-Wah-Tay Station and dumped its coal load down the embankment. It became affectionately known as the 'Coal Mine', where locals would retrieve a few hunks of coal for their 'Quebec' heaters during the 1940s. Groceries were brought up by train from Whitney and Tillie kept a cow in a pasture nearby for fresh milk, butter and cream.

In the summer of 1897, Tillie's younger sister Ida decided to come for a visit, and met the dashing Rock Lake Station Agent William McCourt. Though only 16 years of age to his 29 years, she was instantly smitten, and married him in 1899 in the little white Anglican Church in Whitney. By then there was a station house at Rock Lake, so the young couple lived there until Billie was able to refurbish a log building that he bought in 1901 from the clerk of the Barnet Lumber Company which was operating in the area. It was located across the tracks opposite the Gulland water stand. It was a 16 foot by 24 foot house with an attic, and back lean-too for a kitchen, a 16 foot by 16 foot living room and two 8 foot by 8 foot bedrooms located on the lake side. Ida and Billie used one bedroom and later Ida's mother and father, who moved in with them used the other. Over the years he added an east wing and enlarged the verandah on the front and added a second kitchen out the back. The McCourt's had three children; Oriole (born in 1900, named after another one of Captain William's ships and known as Ory), Myrtle (born in 1902 and known as Matie) and Vernon (born in 1907 and known as Vernie).

Grand Turk Locomotive c 1905

Arriving locomotive c 1910

Oriole, Myrtle and Billie McCourt (L-R) outside Rock Lake Station #1 c 1905

Section Railway gang inspecting the track with local children tagging along c 1910

Mrs. Myers (original Rock Lake resident) waiting for the train c 1920

Section House and Shawna Lodge c 1910

Rock Lake Station with water tower c 1930

Baulke family winter outing

Billy Baulke (L) and sons cutting ice c 1920s

Baulke cottage with resident cow in winter

Billy Baulke hauling ice c 1920s

Campers arriving from train c 1918s

Women fishing c 1918s

Tillie Froebel with unknown local friends and neighbours on gas car c 1910

Myrtle McCourt showing off her new bloomers c 1930

Teenage Myrtle paddling her birch bark canoe

Oriole McCourt at Pen Lake Dam c 1945

Olga Newman with McCourt grandchildren Myrtle (L), Oriole (R), and Vernon (C) c 1908

Grandma Olga Newman

Tillie Froebel (L) and Ida McCourt c 1890

Ida McCourt (L) with daughter Myrtle (R) c 1908

The McCourt Family Roots[12]

According to grandson Robert Taylor, the McCourt family roots in Canada date back to the early 1800's when a number of Irish Quaker families, including the McCourt family, came to Canada seeking a better life. They settled around Frenchman's Bay, Ontario. Born around 1837, Captain William Haney McCourt grew up to be a ship's captain and sailed many ships that plied Lake Ontario between Whitby and Kingston. The cargoes were mostly grain and lumber, which was carried to Kingston in ships with exotic names such as Lavinia, Letitia and Oriole. They would return to Whitby with limestone, which was used to build local buildings including the Whitby Post Office. Captain McCourt also reportedly had a fleet of stone-hookers (a two-masted schooner used for gathering limestone from the floor of Lake Ontario). During the winter freeze-up, the ships were hauled out at Frenchman's Bay and Captain William would spend the winter as a night watchman in the Whitby Town Hall.

In 1862 Captain McCourt, at the age of 25, met and married a young girl, aged 15, named Sarah Wright. Sarah's father, an Englishman named Salisbury Wright, had come to Canada from Yorkshire England with his two brothers and a sister. Family records indicate that he spent his youth as a road builder in Quebec in the early days of the 1837 Papineau-McKenzie Rebellion. But 1846 found him in the fishing business at Frenchman's Bay with a fishing shanty on the east side near a hamlet called Fairport. His favourite fishing location was 'shoal point' which is still well known today. There he met and married a woman named Jane and had four children. In 1862 the Wrights left Fairport for Whitby and soon after daughter Sarah met and fell in love with "Captain William". Together they lived in a large home at the corner where Brock Street (now Hwy 12) interchanges with the Toronto 'On Ramp' of Highway 401. The McCourts raised nine children including Helen, Letitia, William John, Thomas, Ann Elizabeth, Eva, George, and Frederick. As was the custom of the day, in their later years, around 1878, Salisbury and Jane had moved in with William and Sarah. Jane died in 1884 and Salisbury died in 1906. Captain William died on the job at age 75 in 1912. Both Salisbury and Captain William lie in the St. John's (Bay) Anglican cemetery at the Port of Whitby in unmarked graves.

---

12. McCourt Family history provided by Rock Lake resident Robert Taylor, 2003

Booth-Fleck house as seen in Canadian Architect and Builder Review c 1900

Original Booth-Fleck House c 1920

Oriole (L) and Myrtle (R) McCourt aboard the "Opeongo" c 1910

Timber Rights and Patented Land

Previous to the building of the OA&PS railway, J. R. Booth had obtained water and timber rights for 7000 acres of land around the east side of Rock Lake. The area extended all the way up to Rose Pond, included the islands in the middle of Rock Lake, (later named Rose and Jean after his granddaughters), and part of the west shore of Rock Lake. It also included Gordon Lake where a boathouse was built to house a boat that was used when fishing in the area. Later, around 1911 when Nightingale and Lawrence townships became part of Ålgonquin Park, it is believed that Booth exchanged this vast acreage for patent title (i.e. ownership) to 700 acres on the eastern shore of Rock Lake. Unfortunately, according to John Trinnell in his Booth biography, in his will Booth instructed that all of his personal papers be destroyed so the details of this transaction have been lost to history.

His marriage to Gertrude Roselin Seybold, who came from a long-standing Ottawa family, produced eight children. Unfortunately J. R. outlived all but three; Helen Gertrude, John Frederik and Charles Jackson. Helen Gertrude Booth married her father's second-in-command Andrew Walker Fleck, and with him had four children; Bryce (who caught tuberculosis and spent much time at Rock Lake), Gordon (for whom Gordon Lake was named who later took over the J. R. Booth Lumber Company), Rose (for whom Rose Pond and Rose Island were named) and Jean (for whom Jean Island was named).[13]   According to granddaughter Joan Barclay Drummond, Gertrude Booth Fleck was very active in the Ottawa community and established the first day nursery in Ottawa in the Byward Market area on George Street (which still exists today).

Called Men-Wah-Tay Lodge, meaning 'Place of Sunshine', the original house must have been commissioned by Fleck in the late 1890s as photographs of it were featured in 'Canadian Architect and Builder' magazine in 1900. The original architect was W. H. Watts.[14] In addition to the house there was a stable with an attached blacksmith shop for making spikes, grinding axes and fixing horseshoes. By the water, on the north side was a single slip log launching spot with a tall flagpole.[15] Close by was the family's private railroad siding and train station that he called Men-Wah-Tay Station. The original small shelter was replaced in 1920 with a large building on the curve (lakeside) just past the private siding that became the caretaker's residence. The station did not have any call letters as Rock Lake Station did, because there were no telegraph facilities and it was not staffed with a station agent.

The Flecks' would arrive in their private rail car 'Opeongo' that would be parked at the Booth private railroad siding. This siding, located on the hill side of the tracks, was long enough for the 'Opeongo' and a boxcar, which was used to bring up a bull to service the five cows that the family had on the premises. Mrs. Fleck loved that railroad car, and local rumour had it that she had her dining room in Ottawa outfitted to match the interior of the railcar including the arched roof.[16] In addition to Rock Lake, Mrs. Fleck also loved visiting the USA and would upon occasion use the 'Opeongo' to go to Atlanta and Atlantic City. Later when the railcar disappeared, with it went all of the china and monogrammed silverware.[17]

[13.] According to Joan Barclay Drummond, Fleck's granddaughter, most maps of Rock Lake have the islands named incorrectly. In fact the larger island is Rose Island and the one with the sand spit is Jean Island.

[14.] 'Canadian Architect and Builder' Volume 13 - November 1900.

[15.] The current Booth Rock Lake trail runs between the old garbage dump and the stables.

[16.] Her house was eventually restored by a religious group in the 1980s and then bought by the Algerian Government in 2000.

[17.] Repeated attempts by the Drummonds to discover if the car still exists have failed. It is likely that the cost to operate became so high that the car was turned over to the CNR and eventually finally scrapped and removed from the CN Roster.

Until her death, when she arrived at Men-Wah-Tay Mrs. Fleck would descend from the railcar and climb aboard a stoneboat sled on which was nailed a wicker chair. Billy Baulke, the resident caretaker would stow the luggage, take up the reins and the horse, named 'Nellie', would transport her through the woods to the house that sat by the lakeside about half a mile away. Baulke had been a carpenter by trade, hired by Booth to help build the house, and had stayed on with his wife Gertrude, the daughter of the Park Superintendent George Bartlett. Sitting on a mass of bedrock, the house had an enormous balcony surrounding the house on three sides with a huge iron fire escape that hung from the second floor. According to Joan Barclay Drummond it was great for sneaking out at night. There were beaded curtains going into the living room, and gaslights throughout, turned on by a twist of a tap that hissed before the matches lit.[18]

The Flecks always had a great entourage of guests, staff and relatives and if it was wild strawberry or blueberry time, the train would stop at nearby favourite picnicking spots on the way up. Everyone would get out and pick away, until the brakeman would announce that it was time to re-board the train. When in residence, a daily ritual was for Billy Baulke to take Mrs. Fleck on a fishing expedition in her rowboat. As Joan Barclay Drummond, granddaughter of Helen Gertrude Fleck, fondly remembers:

"Every afternoon, weather permitting, would find Granny Fleck sitting in the stern of the "Happy Hour", her lovely double-ender rowboat, on a wicker chair with the legs sawed off. Billy would row her around the lake, cigar in mouth. Three puffs and one spit were his routine with that cigar! The spit because naturally Mrs. Fleck wouldn't catch anything until Billy had spat on her bait or tackle. There they discussed all sorts of worldly matters, while Granny, in her Dr. Locke boots, 'Queen Mary' dress, chocker, hat and gloves, had her line bated and fish dehooked by Billy."[19]

One of the early advantages of the arrival of the railway was the resulting ease of taking logs out of the bush. No longer did lumber companies have to wait until the spring runoff. But more importantly, they were able to build sawmills near their timber limits and transport the resulting lumber out by rail. According to various mentions in leasehold records

[18.] Recollections from Rock Lake resident Joan Barclay Drummond 2004.
[19.] Recollections from Rock Lake resident Joan Barclay Drummond 2004.

at the turn of the century, four other lumber companies operated in the Rock/Whitefish area in addition to the Booth Lumber Company. These included the Barnet Lumber Company, the Jamieson Brothers Lumber Company, the St. Anthony Lumber Company and the McRae Lumber Company. While working for the Barnet Lumber Company, who were logging in the area of Rock Lake Station, a man named James Avery had built a two-story square log house adjacent to Billie McCourt's log cabin. In 1903, after Barnet had logged out the area the company had no need for the building and sold it to McCourt. This building became "Shawna Lodge", which according to the McCourt family meant 'Happy Times' in the Algonkin language.

For visiting friends, mealtime in the 1910s at Shawna Lodge was a five-star affair. After ascertaining the number of guests and the extent of their hunger, Ida would suggest to Billie McCourt that he meander up to the upper bay of Rock Lake to bring in a certain number of lake trout. Usually within half an hour he'd be back with the precise number requested. In addition to the pan-fried lake trout, the meal consisted of potatoes, peas or beans or carrots from the garden and the daily home made Chelsea buns or bread. Naturally dessert was blueberry pie with hand-cranked vanilla ice cream. Ida was very much against strong drink and frowned upon Billie enjoying a glass of good Canadian whiskey or scotch so the beverage of choice was Rock Lake water. Billie used to hang a cup permanently on the stern of his DISPRO to sample the lake's finest when out on an expedition. In those days, the only way to keep things cool was to use ice. The local icehouse contained 3-foot thick ice blocks packed in sawdust that had been cut from Rock Lake during the winter. For the local children it was a marvelous treat to get the large ice chips to eat on a hot day.

By 1904 Booth had tired of railways or had deemed them to be unprofitable, and sold both the OA&PS and Canada Atlantic Railway to the Grand Trunk Railway. To his chagrin, within a few years of the sale, Depot Harbour became one of the commercial gateways to markets in the United States linking to both Ottawa and Toronto via Scotia Junction. This meant that large numbers of freight trains used the line, carrying goods, grain, and other products to and from points east and west.

By 1910, Rock Lake Station was a busy place. History indicates that up to six trains a day passed through, two of which were passenger trains. Over 120 loads of grain a day from the Canadian west would pass through during the summer. During the early years of WWI the line was also used to transport troops to eastern ports.[20] In other locales in the Park, the Grand Trunk Railway had built high-end resorts to attract tourists. These included the Highland Inn at Cache Lake, Nominigan Lodge on Smoke Lake, and Minnesing Lodge on Burnt Island Lake. In addition to being a transportation hub, where steam locomotives were supplied with water, Rock Lake Station had also evolved into a major camping and fishing area. Tourists interested in escaping from the city for a less-expensive summer vacation would come from all over the northeastern portions of Canada and the USA. For women, the dress of the day was not the long dresses common to visitors to the Highland Inn at Cache Lake. Female campers wore breeches and high leather camping boots with colourful jackets and large hats.

For everyone in the local area, the arrival of the train was a highlight of the day. Instantaneously the train platform would become a beehive of activity with people, produce and equipment coming and going on and off the train.[21] As the local telegraph agent, it didn't take Billie McCourt long to realize that there was money to be made from this burgeoning tourist trade. So, after the family moved into "Shawna Lodge", he turned the original log homestead into a grocery and outfitting store to cater to the new campers and fisherman. But Billie still had his job as the Rock Lake station agent earning $1 a day and had to work seven days a week, so he convinced his daughter Myrtle to run the store. Billie was pro-education, so his incentive for Myrtle was that she could keep any of the American currency that the store brought in for her education. She was eventually able to earn enough to go to Queen's University, where she studied languages.

Billie's store was one of the first 'outfitters' of the day, renting canoes, paddles, life jackets and camping supplies to visiting campers. The groceries were several notches above other places, and hand-made ice cream was a visitor favourite. Naturally bait and tackle were available. One year a barrel of apples from the Niagara district arrived by express baggage. In it was a note from a special picker who asked for a return letter and advised them that the barrel had been specially picked so that each apple was exactly the same size. He must have had a special interest in Rock Lake as he'd apparently taken an entire Sunday to pick the 'special barrel' for Rock Lake

---

[20.] *Algonquin*, by Rory MacKay and William Reynolds page 45.
[21.] Recollections from Rock Lake resident Robert Taylor 2003 and 2004.

in Algonquin Park.[22] As the local Park Ranger was later to report:

> "*I have heard many complaints in regard to the difficulties of obtaining fresh milk and the necessities of life. In fact some of the tourists are threatening to abandon Rock Lake altogether. A store in a small way would be of great accommodation and it would assist materially in making Rock Lake a more flourishing resort.*"[23]

In 1915, the Ontario Legislature passed the Park Act that expanded the size of Algonquin Park to include eight new townships on the south and east sides. According to a map compiled and drawn by Ontario's Chief Geographer's Office in 1946, the two on the south edge of the park (Nightingale and Lawrence) that included the Rock Lake area had been added in 1911 and the other six townships on the eastern side of the Park (Edgar, Bronson, Barron, Stratton, Guthrie, and Master townships) were added in 1914. Under the terms of Park Act of 1915 the Ontario Department of Lands and Forests (DLF) took over administration of the area. Its regulations 'forbade anyone to locate, settle upon use or occupy any part of the Provincial Park exceptions being possible under the Regulations.'[24] In the short run the point was moot as all of the settlers, i.e. the permanent residents, of Rock Lake were employees of the railroad and had built their residences on property patented by the railway. However in 1915 the railway deeded much of that land, except that which was expressly needed for the train station, to the government. McCourt thought 'Shawna Lodge' might be useful to the DLF as a shelter hut and proposed selling his buildings plus the 15-acres surrounding it to the crown. It is not clear if McCourt realized that his house was not sitting on land to which he had title. Family lore suggests that before the Park had been expanded to include the Rock Lake area, McCourt had filed a 'Settlers Claim' for 200 acres, which included all lands south of Rock Creek to Rock Lake including the Rock Lake campsite No. 1 and back to the second ridge to the northeast. As those knowledgeable about the history of Ontario land settlement policies will know, when land was 'opened for location' all squatters could enter claims

---

[22.] Recollections from Rock Lake resident Robert Taylor 2003 and 2004.

[23.] This specific comment was actually made in 1929 in a letter to W. C Cain, Deputy Minister for the DLF from Park Superintendent, J. W. Millar after Billie's store had closed. However similar comments were repeated periodically in DLF correspondence until 1947 when the railway was finally shut down.

[24.] McCourt lease correspondence 1916, Algonquin Park Museum Archives.

to 200 acres of land upon which they were sitting. To get patented title settlers had to clear fifteen acres, erect a habitable house and live in it at least 6 months each year for five years.[25] McCourt's claim was denied, as these townships were never officially 'opened' but as the Deputy of Mines wrote at the time."

> *"Unless the railway has parted with some of these lands, I am unable to see how McCourt can claim title. [But] the ongoing question is one of whether or not the Department should take means to evict all of the people [who are living] at Rock Lake, or should they be allowed to remain there and occupy the house, which they claim upon their paying the Department a reasonable rent. There is no question of their having any legal right to the land upon which they live, as the Department has steadily and for years refused to entertain any applications [for such use. However] we ought not to be too rigorous in dealing with the people who had squatted there before the territory was added to the Park."[26]*

It was decided that relationships with those on what was now crown land needed to be worked out on a case-by-case basis. Eventually McCourt's 'claim' was reduced to a one-acre parcel and a 21-year renewable lease eventually issued in 1921. The one-acre parcel ran 330 feet along the railway including halfway up the hill behind the buildings. As use of land seemed more valuable than ownership at the time, this proposal seemed acceptable.

Men-Wah-Tay Station c 1930s

Men-Wah-Tay Station c 1930s

[25.] The Night the Mice Danced the Quadrille by Thomas Osbourne, pg. 151
[26.] McCourt lease correspondence 1915, Algonquin Park Museum Archives.

Melba McCourt on the family Fairmont Motor Car c 1950

Resting for a spell outside the McCourt grocery store c 1910

Bille and Ida McCourt c 1920

Section gang cutting wood

View looking north up and across Rock Creek c 1920

Waiting for the eastbound passenger train c 1910

Rock Lake Station #2 c 1940

Shawna Lodge c 1910

View of McCourt boathouse and Eva Elm's cottage c 1910

William Elms and Eva McCourt Elms outside their new cottage c 1925

Oriole's Cabin on McCourt's Island 1920s

The First Leaseholds

By the mid 1920s Superintendent Bartlett's promotion of the Park as tourism destination at the Canadian National Exhibition in Toronto and in newspapers and magazines in eastern United States began to have an effect. Many of the 'tourists' who had come to Rock Lake to camp got interested in obtaining leases on which to build fishing camps and/or summer cottages. The first to take advantage of the availability of leases were Billie McCourt's sister Eva and his son Oriole. Oriole took out a lease on the small island on the south end of Rock Lake in 1921. In 1925, Billie McCourt's sister Eva Richardson Elms took out a lease on a parcel on the east shore. Later in the 1940s, her son George Elms, a retired air commodore group captain in the Royal Canadian Air Force, would solidify the family's reputation as renegades. He owned a Seabee airplane and would fly up from Ottawa, land on Rock Lake, and tie the plane up to a barrel just off of his dock. One year he brought up from Ottawa a hydroplane to which he attached Willard Taylor's 11 horse power Fleetwin engine. With it he was able to achieve speeds of up to 35 miles per hour. Later in the 1950s when he heard the Department of Lands and Forests was tearing up an abandoned rail line into Galeairy Lake, he bought the rails and built a small railway at his cottage which he used to get his boat, "Eagle Beak", a red Mullins Marine inboard out of the water each fall.

Other arrivals to the area in the mid to late 1920s were the occupants of nine new leaseholds. These included Willis Myers, a school teacher from Ottawa; Henry James Taylor, a business owner from St. Catharines; William Pretty, from Toronto; Rev. Charles Zorbaugh, a minister from Cleveland Ohio; Dr. W. Watson, a doctor from St. Catharines; Dr. William Merritt, an engineer also from St. Catharines who helped build the Welland Canal and Fred Bonsor, an engraver from Toronto who designed the metal plates used to print currency. There were also three families on Whitefish Lake including; Dr. Frances Seybold, a dental surgeon from New York State, Dr. Bruce McCallum, a professor of medicine at the University of Toronto and George Jamieson, owner with his brother Eldred of Jamieson Bros. logging company.

Rev. Charles Zorbaugh arrived at Rock Lake in 1920 and named his site "Indian Clearing" after he discovered a collection of Indian artifacts nearby in an area of dense cedars and swampy deadfalls about 125-150 feet back from the water's edge. The first group of the artifacts included 31 pits, all about 11 inches to 16 inches in depth that were lined with water-rolled rocks. Most (29) of the pits were circular, ranging from a little over 4 feet to 7 feet in diameter. The rest (2) were rectangular, measuring 10 feet by 7 feet and 11½ feet by 6 feet. The rocks lining the pits averaged 6 inches to 22 inches in diameter.[27] Later excavation by a team of archeologists from the University of Toronto, of one of the pits revealed a blue glass trade bead, several small portions of clear lacquered and unlacquered clay pipe stem (one bearing the hallmark "Montreal"), a piece of ground and pecked gabbro rock which may have been an unfinished implement, two small pieces of iron and a small rectangular whetstone, cut and bracketed for insertion into some type of handle. The artifacts suggested that the pits had been used post 1600 A.D.

Zorbaugh also found camouflaged by underbrush and tree cover, up a steep hill at an elevation of about 100 feet above the lake behind the cottage, a cluster of 42 low rock cairns all situated within a radius of 160 feet of each other. Moss covered most of the rocks and some had as many as nine rocks piled one on top of each other and were nearly 20" tall.[28] Though interesting and a source of wonder to the local residents, it wasn't until 1939 that Rev. Zorbaugh was able to generate any interest amoung archeologists. Even that may well have been among coincidence as a team of them were excavating a late prehistoric campsite on the sandy beach when Rev. Zorbaugh convinced them one afternoon to come and visit his 'Indian Clearing'.

Because it was wartime, the site was promptly forgotten about until 1962 when William Noble and a team of archeologists from the University of

[27.] *Ontario Archaeological Society*, Publication No. 11, June 1968 by William Noble pgs. 49-58.
[28.] *Ontario Archaeological Society*, Publication No. 11, June 1968 by William Noble pg. 59.

Toronto were able to obtain funding to excavate, map and document the site in detail. In addition, the group were directed by the child of a local resident to three boulders that sat just off of the nearby Pen Lake portage trail. Two of the boulders were about 200 feet apart and the third was on the east side of the river just down from the Pen lake Dam. On them were six simple, pecked and scratched petroglyph designs, some simple linear strokes and others with curvilinear lines. One resembled a walking snake and another looked like a stylized 'Thunderbird'.[29] In his 1968 report, Noble suggested that the cairns were thought to be of native origin, he and his researchers were unable to determine their use or purpose. Their best suggestion was that they might have been 'tobacco drops' or dedication cairns erected to a guardian spirit after a successful vision. The pits on the other hand, he believed were 'vision pits', constructed and utilized during aboriginal socio-religious rituals, which were an integral part of the life-way of many Algonkin speaking Indian bands'. As he indicated:

"Vision quests were usually performed in an isolated area from the social group and entailed a fast. Under such conditions it is not improbable that psychological inducements in the nature of the visions would occur. They were usually undertaken by a single individual but sometimes in small groups. While the main and perhaps original concept of the quest was part of an initiation ceremony conducted at puberty, late historic accounts indicate that it was also undertaken during many major crises in late life. In general, males were the primary participants, but females are also known to have pursued vision quests. They were large enough for only one or two individuals."[30]

Another early addition to the Rock Lake community was Henry James Taylor (unrelated to Robert Taylor). According to the family logbook, Taylor first came from St. Catharines to fish in Algonquin Park in late teens or early 1920s. Rock Lake was his favourite destination and Dan's Point his favourite camping spot. (Daniel May a guide and one of the original park temporary rangers first cleared room for a campsite there with Peter Thompson, the Parks first Superintendent, on his exploratory trip in 1893.)[31] In 1917 Taylor decided to get a lease and built a cabin in 1921 on the island opposite Dan's Point. The Taylor family played a major part

---

[29.] *Ontario Archaeological Society* Publication No. 11, June 1968 by William Noble pgs. 59-61.
[30.] *Ontario Archaeological Society* Publication No. 11, June 1968 by William Noble pg. 62.
[31.] *Algonquin Story* by Audrey Saunders pg. 101.

in the early development of the community as not only did other family members take out other leases on the lake but also many leaseholders could claim their Park roots from having visited the Taylors on Rock Lake.[32]

Meanwhile, located on a small point near the south end of Whitefish Lake, George Jamieson, one of the Jamieson Brothers, built a cottage and icehouse in 1922. He didn't apply for a "License of Occupation" for the parcel until 1924 because he felt that the cabin, or office as he called it, was part of his timber limit license. However the park officials' view was that he had built the cabin as a summer cottage for his family and that it had never been used in connection with the lumbering operations. After much correspondence a 'License of Occupation' was finally issued in 1931 to George's brother Eldred Jamieson of Ottawa. It was used infrequently and in 1935 was sold back to the Crown. It sat empty until 1939 when it was rented to Miss Wilma Rouse of Ohio who was a friend of Ida McCourt. She was a single lady, in the 'Grande Dame' tradition. For years she worked as the hostess at the Bigwin Inn near Huntsville. On Whitefish Lake she held tea parties, and enthralled visitors with tales of her travels in Europe as a young lady. She had a big cowbell she would ring if she needed the help of neighbours. She also used to make small ornamental bundles of birch twigs that were kept in a basket by the fireplace and used to start fires.

Another early leaseholder was Dr. Watson, who arrived in 1924. He must have been interested in art since he arranged for his brother-in-law (who was reputed to be connected to the now famous 'Group of Seven') to paint a huge landscape mural on one wall of the cabin and had another painting mounted on the back of one of the cabin doors.[33] There is also some suggestion, though no evidence ever uncovered, that Dr. Watson was also connected in some way to University of Toronto's Madawaska Club. This group of friends were all professors at the university who decided in late 1898 to set up a " Summer Settlement" for students and researchers. At one point the group gave considerable thought to settling at Rock Lake. When A. W. Fleck heard this he threatened to exercise his timber rights and log the entire area, including Rose and Jean islands. The members of the club allegedly got so upset that they left the area and chose Go-Home Bay on Georgian Bay. They did however keep the Madawaska name, which the club still has to this day.

[32.] Recollections from Rock Lake resident Peggy Sharpe, granddaughter of Henry James Taylor.
[33.] Notes from research done by Rock Lake resident William Greer 2004.

Another arrival to Rock Lake Station in the 1920s, a community member of a dubious sort, was a disabled veteran from WWI named Walter Pye. For years he camped on the north side of Rock Creek near the river across the field from the station. He later built a ramshackle cabin on the site and in May 1926 applied for a lease. In those days it was important to the DLF that only persons of 'good character' be issued leases. Though Pye listed his occupation as that of a disabled veteran, according to the local ranger James McIntyre the reality was of a completely different sort. According to Ranger McIntyre's report to the Park Superintendent:

> *"Pye is an athlete, can swim, play baseball, run foot races, paddle canoes and drink moonshine in altogether too liberal portions and is overly fond of the weaker sex. He is a married man but his wife left him and returned to England 2 years ago."*[34]

Even with this report, for whatever reasons, the Superintendent was inclined to be charitable, and nearly issued a lease in the summer of 1927. Then he received notice that Pye had apparently died the previous March, so he was relieved of any required action and repossessed the cabin on the site. Later that summer, a rumour surfaced that Pye was in the Park and was in the process of removing articles from the cabin including his bed, and a canoe. Ranger McIntyre came to investigate, and found the door wide open with quite a number of things missing. The authorities were up in arms and issued the closest that the DLF ever got to a 'Wanted Poster'. It was a notice that Pye 'was a trespasser on the property and would be treated as such should he venture onto the property again.'[35]

The last of the early settlers on Rock Lake included the Ebingers and Robbs from Ohio and the Johnstons from Ottawa. Though nothing is known of the Johnston's connection to Algonquin Park, Robb was well known and liked by park staff due to his yearly practice of dropping off cases of 'Chesterfields' [cigarettes] which were handed round to those at Park Headquarters. Rev. Leo Ebinger, though born in Ohio in 1886 had met William McCourt when at an Ottawa pastoral church. His daughter Vida had been ill and McCourt had thought that the pure fresh air at Rock Lake might help her recover. In the early years the Ebinger family stayed at one of McCourt's rental cabins and later was one of the first renters at the

---

[34] Stringer Lease correspondence 1920's, Algonqin Park Museum Archives.
[35] Stringer Lease correspondence 1920's, Algonquin Park Museum Archives.

Baulke's cabins. As his grandson Robert Holmes reminisced:

> "*My grandfather Leo liked the area so well that he returned year after year [inviting both his father David Sr. and brother David Jr. and their respective families to join them]. His brother David Jr. who ran the family business EBCO (Ebinger Sanitary Manufacturers Company) took out a lease on Rock Lake in 1929. His cottage became known for the elaborate fixtures that it contained that had been made by EBCO. Every year when David Sr. arrived at Rock Lake by train, he brought along considerable freight including steel cots and large 20-foot flat bottom punts that could hold most of the family at one time. In 1934 while preparing to open the cottage David Jr. suffered a major heart attack. Doctors and nurses were flown to the lake from Ottawa, but failed to save him and he died at the cottage at the age of 44. According to local legend, his body was taken to the train station by floating it in its coffin across the lake.*"[36]

To get around up and down the rail line inspecting the tracks and making visits to Park Headquarters on Cache Lake, the railway provided handcars purchased from the Casey Jones Manufacturing Company. The railway wouldn't pay to add motors as they thought that motorizing these handcars was a luxury that was not needed when pumping by hand would do the job just as well. But for the section men a motorized vehicle was very desirable. But they were costly - about a month's wages, for most section men. An alternative was the velocipede. This was a three-wheel pump contraption with one wheel following the outer rail. Billy Baulke would often be seen tootling about on one that the Flecks had bought and given the use of to him. It was a much-improved alternative to the handcars.

However, though not a section man and with little need to go up and down the line, Billie McCourt would not be outdone. He acquired a Fairmont motorcar, which was a platform with steel tires and oak wood-spoked wheels run by a single cylinder gas motor. A belt drove a pulley on the front axle and its top speed was about 10 miles per hour. Billie's grandson, Robert Taylor, can remember sitting on the gas car in the back shed on a wooden Salada tea box thinking he was really somebody. As he recalled fondly in 2004:

[36.] Recollections from Robert Holmes, grandson of Rev. Leo Ebinger 2004.

"We kids had a special toy. We would put it [the old Fairmont gas car] on the rails and I was allowed to take all of the local kids up and down the nearby siding. To go in reverse the spark was cut and if quickly enough connected at the correct instant, the motor would stop and go in reverse. Most of the time we couldn't go out on the main [railway] line as the way was blocked by a speeder that was owned by the local Department of Lands and Forests Ranger, Stewart Eady. Once, however, [the speeder] wasn't there so we decided to go for it and headed to Men-Wah-Tay Station on the Barclay Estate. It was great fun getting there, but when it came time to return, we found that the engine wouldn't go into reverse and we were stuck. We had to push it all of the way back and paid a high price when it derailed, as we got caught and were grounded for a week.*[37]

Later after the trains had abandoned the line in 1947 and up until the rails were lifted, the Fairmont gas car was also used by the McCourt family for many berry-picking expeditions to the end of the line at Lake of Two Rivers. As Robert Taylor remembered in 2004:

"First we would traverse the 'Snake' where the line was washed out at Whitefish and the rails were suspended 6 feet above the water, and continue on past the old Wye. This was the place where the locomotives turned for the return trip to Whitney. The curve out and grade was so steep that the locomotives could only back in and would almost fall out the lower leg of the Wye if they weren't careful. A [hand thrown] switch provided the route to the McRae Mill on Lake of Two Rivers. Unfortunately there were only a few lengths of rail so within a few hundred feet we would run through some alder bushes and off the rails into the mud at the end of the branch line."

By 1927 McCourt had a nice little commercial business in operation at Rock Lake Station. In addition to the store and renting half of 'Shawna Lodge' each summer, he also rented out the nearby buildings on what was known as the 'Barnet Property' to visiting tourists. These buildings, located across the tracks from Shawna Lodge, included what was known as the 'Barnet Cottage' and an old warehouse built by the Jamieson Brothers that McCourt had fixed up. The Jamieson warehouse was rented to some

---

[37] Recollections from Rock Lake residents Robert Taylor and Fred Allan Jr. 2003 & 2004.

nurses from Ottawa in 1926 and the Barnet Cottage was rented to Leo Ebinger in 1927. Unfortunately no portion of the resulting revenues ever made their way back to the government coffers as unbeknownst to the renters, McCourt didn't have permission to use any of the Barnet buildings. Soon after this one of the railway employees reported that he'd been paying McCourt rent for using the nearby meadow as pasturage. Apparently at one point there were five cows pasturing on the Barnet property for which McCourt had been charging $1 per head per month. McCourt found himself by 1928 in a mess of hot water.

His troubles had all begun a few years earlier when he had been found tapping the Government telephone line. His version of the story, as found in the archival correspondence, was that:

"He had his own little telephone system between the store and the house, [and that] he had connected his telephone with the Government line for the purpose of calling the doctor at Whitney and intended to remove the connection right away."[38]

Unfortunately, the DLF felt that his explanation did not at all suffice as the ranger's cabin was 'but a stone's throw from his own house and if an emergency existed was open to him to use without cost.'[39] This latest funny business was the last straw, and after much correspondence McCourt agreed to discontinue the carrying on of any mercantile business in the area and would use the buildings on his own lease for private use only for his family.

View of gravel pit arches c 1910 looking north to Whitefish Lake

[38] McCourt lease correspondence 1927, AP Museum Archives.
[39] McCourt lease correspondence 1927, AP Museum Archives.

Rock Lake Station settlement c 1915

Decimated Rock Lake shoreline after a fire c 1910

First Rock Lake Dam c 1917

MacBeth's cabin near Chamberlain Rock

Merritt Chalet Camp 1928

Mrs. Merritt (R) and friend sawing logs 1928

Henry Taylor (later years) c late 1920s

Fishing guide Dan May c 1920

Flora (Taylor) Greer as a young girl 1920

Local Rangers Cabin c 1917

Camping on Dan's Point c 1920

Sitting Henry Taylor (L), Flora Taylor Greer (R), Lisette (Taylor) Pepler (standing)

Taylor cottage 1921

Road into Whitney 1930

Billy Baulke's son Johnny tries out the velocipede c 1920

Shawna Lodge before porch renovations c 1915

Foreman with family in front of Section House c 1915

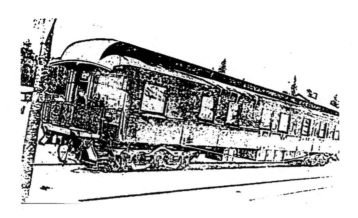

The Beginning of the End of the Railway

By the early 1930s, the Canadian National Railway, which had taken over the operations of the Grand Trunk Railway in 1923, was running only three passenger trains into the Park. The train would come into the Park on Tuesdays, Thursdays and Saturdays and would go out of the Park on Mondays, Wednesdays and Fridays. In 1933, the main trestle at Cache Lake was deemed unsafe and it was decided that repairs would not be made. Local folklore has it that the bridge was felt to be so dangerous by the railway workers that just to be safe the locomotive engineer would stop the train at one end of the trestle. The fireman would get off the train and walk across the trestle. The engineer would then set the throttle and hop off. After the train went across the trestle by itself, the fireman would hop back on, stop the train and wait for the engineer while he walked the trestle and rejoined the train. After the Cache Lake trestle was finally condemned the train coming from the west would stop and turn around at Cache Lake. The train coming from the east would do the same at Lake of Two Rivers. Sometimes the local children were allowed to climb aboard for the turnaround trip. Jake Pigeon, a Cache Lake resident and a young boy at the time, recalls his part-time job:

"There was a turn table for turning the locomotives around. But they didn't turn the whole train around, so the seats had to be turned or flipped to face the other direction. My brother Tom and I used to sweep out the cars and flip the seats and help put the ice into the roof of the cars for air conditioning and climb on top and push the ice down for the drinking water. Our father worked as a ranger during the day and

as a night watchman at the turning station and would stoke the fires with coal to keep the engine going. When we swept the cars we would get [to keep] all of the comic books, odds and ends that were left behind. The comic books were the best because we would only get to town once a month and my mother would give us enough money to go to a movie, buy a chocolate bar or pop and a comic book. The day that comic books went from 5 cents to 10 cents we were devastated. It blew our quarter allowance all to heck. [The campers arriving for] Camp Tamakwa were the best as they left the best comic books behind by far"[40]

In 1933, residents were advised that there was train service twice a week from Ottawa to Rock Lake without any problems. However a growing alternative was to drive to Whitney, leave the car in storage there and connect with a train for Rock Lake that left Whitney at 1:10 p.m. on Mondays or 8:00 a.m. on Wednesdays. As the Park Superintendent wrote:

"The road from Belleville to Whitney via Maynooth is an unimproved dirt, country road from Maynooth to Whitney but is quite passable and gangs are working on it. You could drive that way if you wished as there is considerable traffic over it."[41]

However as resident, John Robb wryly replied:

"I resolved last year that I would never drive to Whitney direct as in previous years. There is too much breakage on my car as a result."[42]

Another alternative was to either motor or take the train from Toronto to Scotia Junction on a Monday or Thursday and connect with the train going east to Algonquin Park Station at Cache Lake. This route required an overnight stay at Bartlett Lodge and the catching the following day of a jitney service that ran east from the foot of Cache Lake along the tracks to Whitney. The schedules though were constantly changing and required confirmation via letter or telegram with the Park Superintendent. Generally passenger trains left Scotia Junction at 3:55 p.m. for the Park on Tuesdays, Thursdays and Saturdays and mixed trains (passenger and cargo) left at 3:55 p.m. on Mondays and Fridays.

[40.] Interview by Don Standfield with Jake Pigeon 1981, Algonquin Park Museum Archives.
[41.] Robb lease correspondence 1934, Algonquin Park Museum Archives.
[42.] Robb lease correspondence 1934, Algonquin Park Museum Archives.

"At present trains from the east get to Rock Lake on Mondays and Thursdays. On Mondays the trains leave at 5:30 a.m. and are due at Rock Lake at 7:45 a.m. On Thursday it connects with a train from Ottawa at Golden Lake at 10:45 a.m. and is due at Rock Lake at 3:45 p.m. A new schedule of trains from the East takes effect on July 14. As yet the agent has not got his new time card so we have no details, but a passenger train is supposed to come up from Madawaska on Saturday evening through Whitney and Rock Lake arriving Rock Lake about 9:30 p.m. This new schedule calls for a mixed train to come up from Madawaska on Tuesdays and Thursdays."[43]

One funny incident happened to Mrs. Merritt who had settled at Chalet Camp on Rock Lake with her husband in 1925. She was under a doctor's care for a stomach ailment, who had prescribed for her a quantity of ale that needed to be taken daily. Her brother Murton Seymour had arranged with the Brewers Warehouse in Huntsville to ship to her, via train, one case of ale every week to ten days. Unfortunately his shipping instructions were not followed and all five cases that Mrs. Merritt was expected to need during her stay at Rock Lake were shipped at once. These arrived at the Algonquin Park Station at Cache Lake and were immediately seized by the Park authorities. At the time, the Park regulations limited the quantity of liquor that could be brought into the Park. Mrs. Merritt was advised that she needed to come to Cache Lake Park Headquarters, along with her residents' permit and the doctor's prescription, sign for the cases herself, and provide an explanation. This was impossible for Mrs. Merritt as neither the train nor the jitney service was in operation and paddling the long distance along the Madawaska River to Cache Lake wasn't feasible. After a flurry of correspondence and telegrams between, Seymour, Merritt and Park Superintendent MacDougall, MacDougall made an arrangement with the local station agent, Mr. Needham and advised Mr. Seymour:

"Each time our gas-car goes down to Rock Lake that the car driver [will] be permitted to carry one case, so that Mrs. Merritt will receive her ale without having to come up and get it and also allow the Park Regulations to be complied with. One case was taken down the first of this week, and the remainder is being delivered as often as the car goes by. There being no train service between Algonquin Park Station [on Cache Lake] and Rock Lake, you should route future shipments from

---

[43.] Zorbaugh lease correspondence 1934, Algonquin Park Museum Archives.

the East. The use of our gas-car for carrying express to Rock Lake in this instance was only given as a courtesy by the CNR in order to assist Mrs. Merritt and not as a regular procedure"[44]

This poor level of train service and odd arrival and departure hours made implementing MacDougall's vision of Algonquin Park as a 'year-round tourist Mecca' a challenge.[45] Several years previously, to try to address the issue, DLF Minister Finlayson announced in 1930, with no public consultation, that a highway would be constructed as a relief project from Huntsville to Whitney through the southern sector of the Park. The initial response from cottagers was very negative. They were concerned that the resulting 'army of motorists would destroy the beauty and tranquility of the Park and would have a detrimental effect on fish and game stocks'.[46]

However by 1933, everyone's perspective had changed. The CNR had announced the closure of the Highland Inn and suggested that they were also going to consider abandoning their southern line through the park completely. This meant that access to cottages and tourist areas would be impossible without a highway. The DLF agreed and by July road survey crews were hard at work and actual construction began in the fall of 1933.[47] Workers were paid $5 a month plus board, and worked six days a week from 7 a.m. to 5 p.m. Two leaseholders, Lorne Pigeon from Cache Lake and Gibby Gibson from Canoe Lake, were part of the work effort. As Gibby Gibson recalled in 1991:

"I worked on that highway doing every possible job that had to be done. I was a bit of a floater so didn't stay too long at any one job which made it pretty good for me. The job that I did the longest was delivering supplies to the camp by boat. I would pick up all of the food and other supplies at Joe Lake Station and then bring it down Canoe lake, into Bonita Lake, through the Smoke Lake Creek and then into Smoke and over to the camp. We used to fill those boats to the gunwales and chug down the lakes fully loaded with sides of beef, vegetables and milk. I used to drop supplies off to the other camps as well. No one ever went hungry at those camps but I made sure that the Smoke Lake camp had the best of everything that was available.

[44.] Merritt lease correspondence 1933, Algonquin Park Museum Archives.
[45.] *Protected Places* by Gerald Killan pg 62.
[46.] *Protected Places* by Gerald Killan pg 60.
[47.] *Protected Places* By Gerald Killan pg 64.

I would do my best to find the supplies required by each camp when I was at the Joe Lake depot. The people at Joe Lake Station all knew me and would pretend to run and hide when I pulled up at the dock. They would be shouting: "Go Away Gibby! We don't have anything for you or your men would want." I would tie up the boat and start talking and eventually work my way into the storehouses and chat with the keeper of the goods. Sometimes it took quite awhile, but I would usually leave with the boat full of supplies waving to the men on shore who would all be lifting their caps and scratching their heads wondering how I once again got what I came for. That boat pretty much knew its way around those lakes by itself. Even at night with just an oil lamp for light we could find our way back through narrow Smoke Creek to the Smoke Lake Camp where we would tie up until the next morning.[48]

Lorne Pigeon's experience was somewhat different.

"The men that had the teams of horses like myself were farmers and worked on the highway slashing and skidding timber in the winter months. We would go back to the farms in the spring and cut wood and work on our farms in the summer and fall and then be looking for employment somewhere again in the winter. I worked at that highway camp from January to March one winter.

I took two horses, Fan and Charlie, from the farm and we walked for two days before we arrived at the camp on Smoke Lake – pretty well where the airplane hangar is today. We pulled a wooden runner sleigh behind the horses that would carry all the supplies needed for the winter months that we would be working in the bush including hay and oats for the horses to eat as well as blankets to cover them during the night. We took enough food supplies for ourselves and also blankets and warm clothes to sleep in once the sun went down and the air started to get brittle. Back in those days we didn't have sleeping bags and some of the winter nights could get a little chilly. We would set up a tarp to shelter ourselves, and the horses making sure there was a fire going most of the night. It could get pretty cold out there after walking all day through the bush and working up a bit of a sweat. You had to make darn sure that the horses didn't overheat and start getting wet because then it would be hard for them to stay warm throughout the night.

[48]. Interview by Don Stanfield with Gibby Gibson in 1991, Algonquin Park Museum Archives.

It was during the depression and I was darn glad to have work. You made $5 a month plus board. When you arrived they gave you a set of working clothes, mitts and boots that you would take care of because you couldn't afford to spend the money you were making on more clothes. Once a month you'd also receive a packet of tobacco and two books of [tobacco] papers. The horses were well looked after and were kept in good stables and received three meals a day. You would be at work at 8am in the morning which meant that the men with the horses would get up around 5am in order to get them ready for the day's work. They would get about an hour to feed in the morning, an hour at lunch and then after the day's work you would feed them dinner and ready them for the night before you [were done and could] go to the cook tent. Sometimes the horses were better looked after than the men. Lunch was always at the main camp so sometimes you had to walk 5 or 6 miles just to get back to lunch.

There were about 100 men in our camp and about 10-12 teams of horses. It took two years off and on to slash out that highway. After those two years it was in no way ready to drive on but had most of the trees cleared and the stumps pulled or burned. Most of the timber from the cut was all burned, not much of it was used for lumber. If the temperature dropped below 35 below zero Fahrenheit then you wouldn't take the horses or the men out to work. The men with the teams of horses would take turns tending the fires so that they didn't go out and that they would burn all night. When you were in camp all day you would play cards, checkers or boil your clothes to clean them so that they wouldn't walk away on their own. Some of the men would bring out their fiddles and play music while we did our chores or chewed the fat.

Every Saturday night would be a bit of a party because we would always get Sunday off. We used to have skating parties, hockey games with blades strapped to our boots and huge bonfires on the ice. We had fantastic cooks. They would set up a big barbeque pit and cook sausage for all the men while they skated and carried on. Someone would have taken off early Saturday afternoon to skid logs out onto the lake so that we would have lots of wood to burn to keep us warm. These fires would throw off enough light for us to see while we were playing hockey. We had to make our own fun but boy did we have a good time. The men would be out there on the ice playing hockey and several other *men would be playing their fiddles around the fires eating sausage and telling stories. The men all got along. I guess we had to in that kind of working and living situation. Just like the loggers out in the bush camps. There was never any theft and very few fights.*

After the slashing, skidding and burning was done, the next stage of the highway was the leveling of the hills and filling in of the holes. This was all done with shovels and wheelbarrows. Two men would work as a team. One on the shovel while the other wheeled the dirt to where it was needed. Then they would switch when the other was tired. Every curve of that highway had thousands of wheelbarrow tracks laid down.[49]

By the spring of 1935 much progress had been made. However, definite forecasts as to when it was going to be completed were impossible. The road crews were constantly being shifted and sometimes reduced. The best that DLF could do was to issue a monthly status bulletin. As the one for July 1935 reported:

"Cars have been coming in to Cache Lake for the past week, although the road is not officially open. From Huntsville to Tea Lake the road has been graded and is in fair shape. From Tea lake to Cache Lake there is grade only. And it is a very rough stretch, and almost impassable after a heavy rain. However, work is going on all the time, and it is gradually being improved, and you should be able to get in by the first of the month without trouble. There are no provisions for gasoline in the Park, so that your tanks should be well filled before leaving Huntsville. There are no facilities for storing cars at this point anywhere in the Park."[50]

Highway 60 officially opened for business in 1936 and during that first year 3,809 cars were checked in through the West Gate. In the early years the 'highway was really not much more than a trail full of crooked ruts. It had lots of low swampy places, sharp curves and abrupt little hills and was maintained by a grader that would pass by three times a week. From Cache Lake to Whitney it was a bit rough but passable except after a heavy rain."[51] The trip from Huntsville to Cache Lake usually took one and a half hours

---

[49.] Interview by Don Stanfield with Gibby Gibson and Lorne Pigeon 1991, Algonquin Park Museum Archives.
[50.] DLF correspondence 1935, Algonquin Park Museum Archives.
[51.] *The Raven*, June 1966 Volume 7 #2 (R.R). It wasn't until 1948 that it was paved.

on a good day and as the Allan family experienced:

> *"We were always intrigued by our mothers' story of driving the new highway as it was being built – the base apparently being logs – with the car shaking and rattling so badly that eventually one of the headlights was shaken right out. The journey continued after a towel was wrapped around the light and it was wedged back in place."*[52]

The route in from Ottawa was even more terrifying. As Hank Laurier remembered:

> *"We lived in Montreal and used to always go to the Gaspé for our holidays. But in 1935 our family doctor felt that mountain air would be better for my brother Carl's allergies so the family decided to send us to [Taylor Statten's] Camp Ahmek on Canoe Lake. That first year we went by train but in 1936, my dad Robert decided to drive us up to camp. It took nine hours to complete the 190-mile journey. The last 85 miles between Golden Lake and Canoe Lake was a single lane road negotiated at an average speed of 20 mph. We were constantly afraid that we might meet another vehicle coming the other way as we approached the crests of hills."*[53]

Though the highway enabled access for many to many Algonquin Park residents, it was of little value for those on Rock Lake and Whitefish until much later when the Whitefish Access Road was completed. What was even more difficult was that Russell White's jitney service, that used to run on the train tracks from Whitney to Canoe Lake Station, was discontinued in May 1936. As Murton Seymour wrote a month later:

> *"If we take the train to Park Headquarters, there is at present no means of getting us to Lake of Two Rivers. If we motor to Two Rivers either we have to come up the day before and stay at Cache Lake overnight or leave St. Catharines anywhere from 2am to 4am depending upon the train we hope to catch. As you can appreciate, taking two days for a trip, which should not take more than 8 or 9 hours, is rather ridiculous. If the DLF were to establish gas car transportation from Park Headquarters to Rock Lake, which I think is a reasonable request under the circumstances, this difficulty would be eliminated."*[54]

[52] Recollections from Rock Lake resident Fred Allan Jr. 2004.
[53] Recollections from Canoe Lake Hank Laurier 1999.
[54] Merritt lease correspondence 1936, Algonquin Park Museum Archives.

The routes leaseholders took into Rock and Whitefish Lakes at the time were many and varied. Some would fly from Huntsville on a floatplane that could land on the lake and would shuttle people in from Limberlost. Others would drive to Lake of Two Rivers and then take the Eastbound train which only departed on Mondays, Wednesdays or Fridays. Others drove to a point near Kearney Lake and would walk a mile in to Whitefish Lake. Billy Baulke would meet the new arrivals in his pointer boat and deliver the leaseholder to their dock. Sometimes if one was lucky or had connections, the Park officials were understanding of these access difficulties:

"There are taxis in Whitney but no regular service. We can arrange to get you down somehow, as our men have cars and will use them as taxis in the event that there is no other service available. Or if the road is impassable, we will get you down by gas car. I can assure you that we have done all we can to try and secure some adequate form of transportation but to date nothing has been done. The present situation will I trust, soon be changed and a better road provided through this area."[55]

Hauling Dirt for Highway 60 construction c 1935

[55] Department of Lands and Forests correspondence 1936, Algonquin Park Museum Archives.

Stewart and Beulah Eady c 1950s

Eady Family c 1950s

Stewart Eady near retirement

Eady Family c 1950

Stewart and Beulah Eady wedding photo 1915

Stewart Eady at Rock Lake Ranger cabin c 1940s

Other New Arrivals

Another new arrival to Algonquin Park in the early 1930s was Stewart Eady and his wife Beulah. The Eady family were originally from Horton, just outside of Renfrew, where Stewart was born in 1893. He married Beulah in 1915 in Eganville, and later moved to Deacon, Ontario near Golden Lake. Together, the Eadys had eight children including; Charlie, Betty, Lloyd, Eldon, Arthur, Donald, Keith and Leah. Stewart's connection to Algonquin Park was an interesting one. As a young man, as was often the custom of the times, Stewart and one or more of his brothers would venture into the Algonquin Park area to do a little illegal trapping. One year, they got caught and Stewart's life was forever changed. After a thorough talking to Stewart, instead of being taken off to jail in Pembroke, was offered a job as a Park Ranger. This job he went on to hold for over 35 years (23 years of which was based at Rock Lake). One of the conventional theories at the time was that a fellow ex-poacher would be better able to 'ascertain the ways and means of their fellow poachers and therefore be better able at catching or stopping their activities.'[56]

Eady accepted the job and his first posting was at Lake Travers. Later, in the early 1940s he was given the territory from Rock Lake to Cache Lake. The family lived in the former double railway section house near Rock Lake Station in summer and in Whitney in winter. His son Eldon could remember catching the train at the Whitefish Iron Railway Bridge and hitching a ride to go to school in Whitney in the spring and fall. According to local legend, Beulah Eady was the only woman who could make bread, pump gas, and collect frogs all at the same time. Her blueberry pies and

---

[56.] Recollections from Rock Lake resident Art Eady 2004.

Chelsea buns were infamous in the local area. As Ruth Welham-Umphrey from Whitefish Lake fondly remembers:

> *"We called them sinkers, because they were so heavy and yeasty, one would sink if one went swimming after eating two of them. But eat them we did. There would always be several missing from the box by the time we [had paddled] back to the cabin."*[57]

One of the main responsibilities of a park ranger in those days was to keep an eye out for poachers. Over the course of his long career Eady caught and brought to justice in Pembroke over 100 trappers. In winter, Eady patrolled for poachers with his dog team, sometimes accompanied by one or more of his sons. One son, Art, has many great memories of going out on patrol with his father:

> *"Once my father and I were crossing Whitefish Lake when we saw three wolves away down the lake chasing a deer out onto the ice. By the time we got to that part of the lake the wolves had killed the deer and run off. The deer was already half-eaten. They would have finished eating it after we left."*[58]

Another story that Art remembers his father told frequently happened when Art was about 14 years old. One sunny afternoon in winter, Stewart had taken a detour to check on what he thought were some strange snowshoe tracks. Art had gone on ahead and was walking up Rock Lake, across the ice, oblivious to the fact that there were four wolves tracking his footprints. When Stewart, who was following far behind, came upon the wolf tracks, he was worried that the wolves may have killed and devoured his son. Luckily the wolves had gotten side-tracked and discovered two deer that they cornered out on the ice. They had totally forgotten Art and Stewart who came upon them eating the deer.

One of Stewart's other favourite stories that he liked to tell children was about the time he had to camp out for the night and could hear the wolves howling close by. He made a bed like a hammock in a tree and slept there until nearly morning. When he awoke he heard a sound under the tree, and looked down to see two wolves with a beaver, trying to get the beaver to chew the tree down for them.

[57.] Recollections from Whitefish Lake resident Ruth Welham- Umphrey 2004.
[58.] Recollections from Rock Lake resident Art Eady 2004.

Some of Stewart Eady's most memorable stories in those years involved catching poachers.[59] One November, on Galeairy Lake, he caught a group who were carrying over $2,000 worth of furs. He was in his motorboat and forced the poachers onto Loon Island and held them there, until other Rangers came. It was too cold for the poachers to swim so they were caught red-handed. On another patrol Eady found a beaver trap in the center of a pond. He staked out a position at one end of the pond and had his son Eldon do the same at the other. There was no escape and they caught the poachers red-handed as they were taking a beaver out of the trap. Another time Stewart came upon a poacher who fell in the water just as he was about to take a beaver out of the trap. The Eadys watched silently in the bushes and when the poacher had taken off his wet pants and boots, moved in and literally 'caught him with his pants down'.

Once when working with Jack Gervais, they gave chase to a fellow who was poaching in the winter with his snowshoes on backwards. This was a common trick so that the Rangers would think the trapper was going the other way. This guy was also wearing a false beard so that he wouldn't be recognized if the rangers did catch up to him. Jack and Stewart followed him a long way, before they confronted him. As Art recalls:

> "The poacher raised his gun and fired. Jack scrambled for cover behind a tree, but tripped and fell on his snowshoes. Stewart known to be a good shot raised his rifle. The poacher yelled out: "I didn't shoot him! I didn't shoot him Stewart! I shot over his head!" Stewart held his fire and the poacher escaped. They never did catch him, but they knew who he was and the poacher knew that they knew. He laid low for a long time after that."[60]

On another patrol, when Stewart was at Lake Louisa, he saw smoke and went to investigate. Later he realized upon reflection that it was a father and son team. When Stewart arrived, only the father was there. The man fired a shot into the air and loudly shouted to Eady that he'd got him, giving his son time to escape. Another incident occurred near Lake of Two Rivers when Stewart heard shooting in the bush. He phoned the West Gate and told them to search every car as two pet deer that were the pets of the Chief Ranger's wife had been shot. They stopped the culprit at the West Gate only to discover that he was the police chief from Huntsville.

[59.] Recollections from Rock Lake resident Art Eady 2004.
[60.] Recollections from Rock Lake resident Art Eady 2004.

There were also great fears on the part of DLF officials that some of the locals were part of the poaching activities. Though rare this was confirmed in one case when one leaseholder advised the Park authorities that:

"These local boys, about 20 and 18 years of age, are first cousins. Their father is a brother of my wife. I do not think that my stepson is the ringleader, but he is always ready to fall in line when someone else proposes a light job, and usually carries the rifle. I do not go up every year [to Rock Lake], as it keeps me busy providing funds for those who do go, but every time I have been up there, I know that deer are being killed for I have been an eye witness. When a deer is killed it is divided up and each recipient is more or less guilty of breaking the laws, leastways are all a party to the deed. I have remonstrated with my wife and stepson regarding the matter, but without success. Now, I do not wish to trouble you further with this matter, I feel that at least I have done my duty in notifying you. I do know also that one of my neighbours is always in terror for fear his boys should get caught as we are the one who would actually suffer [and] we would have to pay the fines. As I wrote before, I am not able to stand for that financially."[61]

Though off the beaten path, and under the watchful eye of the local Park Rangers, their relative infrequent use made Algonquin Park cabins ready vandalism targets. Though vandalism was more often of an animal rather than human sort it more often occured in the spring and fall. Human thieves got organized as they did in 1934 when a ring based in Whitney raided a number of leaseholds on Whitefish Lake. It first came to the attention of the Park authorities that fall, when Dr. Seybold advised the DLF that his cottage had been broken into and the following items stolen[62].

- Two canvas cedar canoes with three good paddles
- A square stern row boat 15 ft and 2 pairs oars
- One large drop leaf table with 6 bow-backed, 2 square-backed and 2 large rocking chairs
- Two iron beds with coil springs with mattresses, one iron cot with mattress, one wood cot with mattress and two small dressers with mirrors and one large trunk with blankets.

[61.] Leasehold correspondence Algonquin Park Museum Archives.
[62.] Seybold lease correspondence 1934, Algonquin Park Museum Archives.

- One set of white porcelain dishes from T. Eaton Co. gold cloverleaf pattern
- Plated silver in a drawer
- One cross-cut saw and one canvas pack

He also indicated that he had heard that his neighbour Dr. G. Andrews had also been broken into. When asked if there was anyone in the area who might have been harbouring any resentments towards him, he recalled an incident 5-6 years previously when he'd hired a guide and former fire ranger named Ruddy to take him on a fishing trip. Seybold hired him without asking the price of the guiding services only to discover upon departing on the trip from the train station, that Ruddy wanted $5 per day rather than the regular $4 per day. Seybold indicated that he thought the regular rate was $4 and asked another guide at the train station if this was so. The other guide indicated that yes in fact that was so and that if Ruddy asked for more he could lose his guiding license. Seybold said that he would pay the $5 but reserved the right to report him. Ruddy accepted the $4 rate but was 'mad clear through'.[63] The DLF replied that:

> *"The Provincial Police immediately investigated, but there was not much to go on except that the culprit wrote on your windows and seemed to know your name. A regular patrol has been kept on the cottages except when the rangers are out chasing poachers and the job was done in their absence. We found in Jamieson's cottage, also broken into, an almost new 16-foot canoe, which Jamieson says, does not belong to him. Did you have a canoe of this description in your cottage? We have it at the ranger's cabin at Rock Lake. They also have a line on a 15-foot canoe, which is outside the Park. This is in the hands of trappers and until we can be sure of our ground and see it quietly or catch them with it we cannot just be sure whether it belongs to the persons who are using it or if it was stolen. I am very sorry about these occurrences and assure you that we are doing all we can to stop them."*[64]

[63.] Seybold lease correspondence 1934, Algonquin Park Museum Archives. Later it became apparent that Ruddy had nothing to do with the break-ins.

[64.] The DLF did later seize the canoe from the trappers who claimed that a tourist had given them it. A reward was given to Ranger McCormick who passed it on to the party who was responsible for its recovery and who wanted his identify kept secret. The party who stole the canoe had not been identified. Seybold lease correspondence 1934, AP Museum Archives.

In the end it turned out that in addition to Andrews, Seybold and Jamieson, two other Whitefish residents, McCallum, and Blatherwick, also had their cottages broken into and items stolen. However the case was solved quite rapidly and in early 1935, the DLF announced that the robberies at Rock and Whitefish lakes had been solved, with the arrest of Michael Worankie who:

> "Turned King's Evidence and today gave Provincial Constable Porter and Chief Ranger McCormick all the information pertaining to the case, who was involved and the disposal of the stuff taken from the cabins. The hiding place is being looked over this afternoon and the stolen goods will be taken to Rock Lake and kept until claimed next summer. Warrants have been issued for the arrest of two other men involved Steve Worankie, and Michael Lavallee. They have been involved in nine robberies since last fall, and we believe yours will be traced to their activities. All the men are from Whitney, Ont. The clue that led to these cases being solved was some printing on the window of Dr. Seybold's cottage.[65]

In March, the DLF closed the case by noting that Steve Worankie was sentenced to two years in penitentiary, Michael Worankie, was given a one year suspended sentence and fined $25 and Michael Lavallee was given one year at Burwash (near North Bay), a year indeterminate and a $25 fine. Seyguin the trapper who had the stolen canoe was given a two-year suspended sentence.

[65.] Seybold lease correspondence 1934, Algonquin Park Museum Archives.

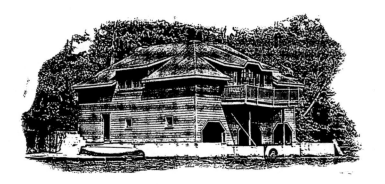

The Fleck Estate Changes Hands

In 1935, Helen Gertrude Booth Fleck sold the original Fleck Estate to her daughter Jean, who had in 1919 married a lawyer, Macgregor Barclay. Known as Gregor, he later become a Quebec judge. Gregor and Jean had two children, Ian (who was born in 1921) and Joan (who was born in 1925). The Barclays would come to Rock Lake every summer alternating two months one year (July and August) and then three months the next (July August and September).

Soon after having the estate to themselves, Jean Barclay decided that the place needed upgrading. Her first impulse was to demolish the original residence, so she hired a leading Ottawa architect of the day named John Ewart to design a new residence. After some thought and investigation, Ewart told her that the main part of the house was in good condition, built on solid rock and that to remove it would be very costly. He suggested an extension of the old building and that it be made two stories high with two wings. Under his direction, the front glassed in pavilion and the porches were removed and replaced with a new extended front and screened in porches on either side on the ground level. On the second level, he proposed that the space over the porches be redesigned as open sleeping areas. The rear of the house was enlarged as well, including the addition of a huge walk-in icehouse, one side to be used for meats and fish and the other side for fruits and vegetables. The room had double walls encased in ice in the summer that kept everything inside perfectly cool. As Joan Barclay Drummond fondly remembered, "The Barclay children had fun during the rebuilding, learning to spread tar and to put on cedar shingles and generally get in the way of all of the workmen."[66]

The Judge was also an avid gardener. According to George Pearson, the caretaker who took over after Billie Baulke retired, Judge Barclay would send up in June all sorts of flowers, such as geraniums and salvias and seeds every year. Even the Pearsons' had a garden and were able to grow potatoes, cucumbers, beans, radishes, onions, chives, mustard and mint. They had to install chicken wire all around it so the deer wouldn't go in and tramp it all down or eat all the young shoots.[67] Flowerbeds that contained day lilies and lilac bushes were added front and back and a huge lawn was added in two levels that extended from the lake to the large patio in the front of the house. Never was there a single weed in those lawns. The Judge would spend hours, kneeling on a straw cushion with a knife in his hand pulling out every stray weed.

A new boathouse was erected for the east side of the property with three sideslips and a large room upstairs with a balcony overlooking the southeast of the lake. The boathouse doors rolled up and down with ropes. The upstairs area of the boathouse had a huge fireplace at one end and a dance floor above the three 5-foot wide boat slips. There was a ping-pong table, hockey game and an old speaker wind up gramophone. Many a happy fun-filled hour was spent up there. It was also used as both a local dance hall and meeting place for local Rock Lake residents, which may well, have caused the permanent sag in the balcony. During WWII a Red Cross group (Whitney Branch) of Rock Lake women, led by Mrs. Barclay and the local park rangers wife (Mrs. Eady) met twice a week for five weeks, sewing and knitting bandages and other needed articles for the war effort. They produced a record 480 items.[68]

The Barclays also hired a Toronto man to design and build a paved double tennis court that he had built on the highest point of land of the Barclay estate surrounded by huge pine trees. It was located on the walking path from the estate main building to the two stone gate pillars at the road entrance by the railway roadbed. According to George Pearson 'the chip stones for the tennis courts were hauled in by train and then rolled into a flat surface with one of those rollers filled with water. We rolled and rolled

---

[66]. Recollections from Rock Lake resident Joan Barclay Drummond 2004.
[67]. Interview by Ron Pittaway with George and May Pearson 1976, Algonquin Park Museum Archives.
[68]. According to an article in the local Whitney newspaper at the time.

and rolled and then put tar on it.'[69] In the building process, a number of Indian artifacts were unearthed and much to daughter Joan's delight a team of archeologists and students arrived from the University of Toronto. They stayed for about two weeks and eventually decided that the site must have been an Algonkin camping ground at one time.

In 1936, after the renovations were completed, Judge Barclay and Jean began to invite friends, relatives and folks from the lake to visit. As Mary Eleanor Riddell Morris recalls:

"As I was fortunate to be up at the lake during my high school and university days, I was often invited over to the Barclays to play tennis in the mornings. By the tennis court there was a little pavilion where drinks and biscuits were served. Often Mrs. Barclay very kindly invited me to stay for lunch served by a maid!"[70]

When in residence, the staff included a person who staffed the business car, sometimes their chauffeur, and a household staff that included three maids and a cook. The staff had full use of the boats and canoes every Thursday afternoon and as the main meal on Sundays was at noon, were also able to use the facilities on Sunday afternoons. For most of the staff, their quarters were on the second floor, complete with their own bathroom facilities including a bathtub but no shower. All of the grey water (including the kitchen) went into a huge septic system. The permanent year-round caretaker's main job was keeping an eye on the place and keeping an eye out for fire when no one was in residence. Judge Barclay was very concerned about fires and put up signs at various choice places around the property and on the two islands. They were white with black lettering on galvanized plates framed with a black wooden border.

> *"No Camping, No Fires"*
> *By Order*
> *Gregor Barclay*

One such sign still exists at Merritt's Chalet Camp on Rock Lake.

[69.] Interview by Ron Pittaway with George and May Pearson 1976, Algonquin Park Museum Archives.
[70.] Recollections from Rock Lake resident Mary Eleanor Riddell Morris 2004.

New Barclay Boathouse c 1930s

New Barclay Main House c 1930s

View of Main Barclay House from dock

Barclay tennis courts

(l to r): (l) Barclay family arrival at Men-Way-Tay station c 1940s, (r) Barclay front lawn and garden looking west

The Main House

The main entrance was at the back on the railway side of the house. Visitors would step up two steps to a front door that opened into a rectangular hall. If one proceeded straight through you entered a large living and dining room. The living room had a large fireplace made of fieldstones located on the east side of the room. North of the living room was a screened in porch that extended on an angle facing the lake, which was primarily used as a games room on rainy days. South of the living room was the dining area with it's 'twin' screened in porch also on an angle facing the lake. Off the dining room was a door to the pantry, which opened into the large square kitchen and maids' dining area. Through the kitchen door and down five steps led to the double-chambered cold storage room and behind that was the icehouse. To the west of the kitchen, facing the lake, were the back stairs which led up to the three maids' rooms with bathroom and a main linen closet on the second floor.

To the south of the main entrance was a multi-level pine staircase that led to a large landing area on the second floor. To the extreme north was a double guest room, facing the north, a single one facing northeast and a bathroom that was over the front door. Down the hall, still going north was a large room in the center of the house known as 'Granny Fleck's Room', which had its own bathroom. To the right of her room was a large room and bathroom with a screened in sleeping porch that was directly over the games room below. To the left of her room was an identical large room and bathroom with a screened in sleeping porch that was directly over the dining area. To the north of the main entrance hallway was another 'wing' with a large sleeping room, bathroom and sleeping porch with very high windows facing north and northeast.

Also off of the main entrance hallway (to the east) was a large square room with no windows that was used as a utility mudroom. Here all the equipment for fishing, tennis, swimming etc. were all kept. At the back of the room was a door with a passageway that ran to the kitchen and basement. In the basement set in concrete and the natural rock foundation was a large double washtub, a wood-fired furnace, a tool room plus the siphon tank that was used to make soda water and coca cola.

[71.] Recollections from Rock Lake resident Joan Barclay Drummond 2004.

Coinciding with the Barclay house renovation was the departure in 1935 of Billy Baulke, who with his family left the Fleck Estate and settled on his own land that he had obtained in 1929. Later known as Baulke's Point, it was located up the shore from the Estate.[72] There are no lease or patent records of this transaction in the archives, so it may be that perhaps Granny Fleck provided Baulke with title or right of access to the land upon which he built his various cottages and provided him with a modest pension for his many years of service. Baulke suggested to the Barclays that George Pearson take over his caretaker duties, which was agreed upon.

With his wife Gertrude, Billy had seven children including Louise, Charlotte, Gertrude, Jim, Morris, Robert and Johnny. He built three cabins on the site that he rented out to tourists at a rate of $65 per month, with $35 extra if the renter wanted to include wood and ice. He also later established a grocery store where he sold groceries, gasoline, and coal oil to the cottagers and milk that he obtained from the Barclay's cows. By request from the other cottagers, Leo Ebinger would hold a church service most Sundays that he was at the lake, which would be held on Baulke's front porch with music provided by a pump organ played by Baulke's wife Gertrude, his daughter Louise (who later became a deaconess) or Ebinger's daughter Elizabeth.[73] In winter he would cut blocks of ice from the lake, aided by his son Johnny. Johnny Baulke later went to work for DLF at Cache Lake and for several years lived at the Smoke lake Hangar. They would store the blocks in the community icehouse located on land between the Louie and Fountain cottages on Whitefish Lake, and many a leaseholder son had a summer job delivering the ice to residents on both lakes.[74] As echoed by many of the Baulke's tenants who went on to obtain leases in the area:

> *"What a wonderful place the Baulke's was for the three summers we rented one of their cabins, with its chicken coop, which was a great place for finding worms, the canoe trippers stopping in at the store to reprovision and Mrs. Baulke not wanting to sell any one person two of anything just in case someone else arrived needing one; the great sand beaches where we learned to swim and dive for clams; Blueberry Hill*

---

72. Now know known as Rock Lake Campsite No. 2.
73. Recollections from Robert Holmes grandson of Rev. Leo Ebinger 2004.
74. According to residents, Johnny Baulke moved to Collingwood to manage Castle Glen a real estate development.

for berry picking; the jigger to hitch rides on once in awhile; the old school house to explore; the railroad tracks to test your balance on when you were out picking raspberries."[75]

Because of a need to educate his growing family, Billy had also worked to establish a school district and obtained revenue for the maintenance of a school at Rock Lake. The one-room school that opened in 1934 was located behind the Baulke cottages up by Rose Pond. It was part of the Haliburton School Board and attendees included Johnny Baulke and the section foreman's children. Mrs. Baulke and later the Park Ranger's wife, Mrs. Eady, were the teachers.

One unfortunate result of the building of a school was the realization by the local municipality of Sherbourne that there were a number of properties in the Rock Lake area that could be added to their tax rolls. They immediately assessed all of the leaseholders municipal taxes for 1934 and 1935. These taxes were double the Provincial Land Tax rate that leaseholders had been paying previously. Since the township of Sherbourne was over 50 miles away, residents got no return whatsoever. This also meant that Rock Lake leaseholders were 'placed in an entirely different position to any other of the park leaseholders which was seen as obviously absurd and unjust.'[76] After much local internal discussion residents demanded from the DLF that they be placed in the same status as all other park leaseholders. By 1936 DLF was not responding so orchestrated by lawyer Murton Seymour; each leaseholder signed a petition asking for the detachment of Nightingale Township from Sherbourne Township. In this they were successful and in 1937 the area became subject only to the Provincial Land Tax[77].

[75.] Recollections from the Allen Family on Rock Lake 2004.
[76.] Department of Land and Forests correspondence 1935 Algonquin Park Museum Archives.
[77.] Merritt lease correspondence 1935-1937 Algonquin Park Museum Archives.

Cottage Building

Cutting down trees to obtain logs for building purposes required permission from the Department of Lands and Forests (DLF) and cost 1¢ per lineal foot for trees under 6" in diameter and 3¢ per lineal foot for trees over 6" in diameter. If you were cutting trees on your own parcel you were expected to own up and submit the required monies. Sometimes though even the best-laid plans ran into trouble as Rev. Charles Zorbaugh found when he arranged to have his cabin built in 1933.

"No doubt you will remember that I engaged Jim Hyland last fall to put up a log cabin for me. As it turned out Jim was unable to do the job so his son Rory undertook it. Perhaps you have heard what sort of a job he did. He must have been drunk all the time. It is absolutely impossible to describe to you the miserable product of his efforts. In the first place, there is no foundation. The bottom logs are already slipping. He evidently picked up odds and ends of logs to throw together and cover with a roof. There aren't two logs the same size in the structure. As a result there are six and even more inches between some of the logs, These places are filled in with odd pieces - just shoved in as chinkers. I don't believe that there are more than three full logs in the building that run the length or width of the building (20' by 12')   The structure is a conglomeration of odd sized pieces. It really def   . As Ranger Bowers said, there isn't a real log in the wh I am greatly disappointed. The only thing I ca torn down and salvage what I can in the wa can save the doors, the lumber in the floor an

the roofing. It will have to be rebuilt from the foundation up. Ranger Bowers is going to try and find a reliable man to do the job for me. It will mean building a new cabin and will require new logs as the present logs are not matched and even a magician couldn't build a cabin out of them.

I realize that to build a new cabin I will require more logs (counting those already used) than such a building would ordinarily require. I [am] wondering if under these unusual circumstances you would permit [me to replace] the cabin, charging me only for the logs used in the [new] structure. I am fully aware that this is a rather unusual request [and would] never suggest it under other circumstances. But the logs now [I] honestly worth nothing and I know that you would agree [that] they were picked up with no reference to their value.

Perhaps I am exaggerating I wish you would call Ranger [Bowers by] phone and ask him what he thinks about it. Of course [this whole] affair is my own tough luck and that you [may think the req]uest unreasonable. If so please do not hesitate for I think that you can see my end of it however. [If torn] down. Additional logs will have to be found.

is extremely low. Should you build your cabin at the average height of eight logs and carry out the uniform plan by having cedar rafters and joists, the total costs will be very moderate indeed. Your doorframes and window sash can be had from the J.D. Shier Co Bracebridge Ont. where all your requirements can be secured at moderate prices." [79]

Because he was a skilled carpenter Baulke and later his son Johnny, were often in demand to build cabins for the newly arrived leaseholders. Others would build their cabins themselves over the course of many weekends and sometimes years. A few got built with whatever was around. When the Steinbergs, took over from Lionel Nelson in 1977, they found that:

"The cottage itself was unique, created from bits and pieces of wood, windows and doors from abandoned leases. As the story goes, the original leaseholder, Lionel and Marjory Nelson, purchased the lot but failed to build on it until the required time line was nearly up. To meet the deadline Nelson busily scrounged materials from around the lake and as a result, no corner was square and no surface was level. The little place certainly had character! Every nook and cranny was filled with piles of someone's treasures including the sleeping loft that contained a multitude of boxes of clothing, shoes, hats, corsets, and purses." [80]

And as Rose Campbell recalls:

"We asked if we could dismantle the cottage and bunkie [from a nearby abandoned lease] and re-use the materials to build a new cottage on our lease. DLF was in agreement as long as the site was cleaned up to their satisfaction. This was quite a feat. With many leaseholders as spectators to watch we dismantled a 34' cabin plus a 10' by 12' Bunkie in sections off a very steep hillside. [We then] transported it down the lake in a 16-foot aluminum boat. That summer was entirely spent clearing the land and erecting the bunkie while living in a dilapidated shack overrun by mice and chipmunks looking for handouts. We were certainly entertained in the evenings by the flying squirrels. One morning, it was quite a laugh, we woke to find that the nose pads of my glasses had been chewed away by one of our unwanted little guests.

---

[79] Department of Lands and Forests correspondence to John Robb 1928, Algonquin Park Museum Archives.
[80] Recollections from Rock Lake resident Helen Steinberg 2004.

The next summer we began building our own cabin by ourselves. No contractors were ever involved. We did this every weekend. All materials needed were transported down the lake by our 16' foot aluminum boat. Lumber we acquired from a mill in Wilno, furnishings acquired via auctions, yard sales, or old stock from home.[81]

Stewart Eady and his sons were also highly sought after by the newcomers for their cabin building skills. They helped Dr. Dunn, a dentist in Orillia build his cabin on the river. He'd bought a Halliday 'Ready-Cut Summer Cottage', whose pieces arrived on a boxcar at Rock Lake Station.[82] Lloyd Eady brought it over and assembled it for them. No expense was spared as the kit even included a three-piece bathroom with hot water, a water pressure system and septic tank. Being an architect, Robert MacBeth had built over the winter a 1 inch to 1 foot scale model of a cottage that he wanted Lloyd Eady to build for him. The Eady brothers cut the logs for him on Louisa Trail and built cribs that were then filled with rocks and sunk. The lower level became the boathouse and the upper level became the cottage and hung out over the water. In the summer of 1950 Howard Jeffery brought his wife Marian, and 5-year-old daughter Judy, to their parcel where they camped in a tent for two weeks while Howard built the original cottage with help from Art and Keith Eady. The cottage had one main room, a kitchen and small bedroom. That November, he and Marian brought the cook stove down the lake in the small cedar strip boat and installed it and the stovepipes. The next year Howard added two back bedrooms. From then on Howard's view of life in Algonquin Park included building something one year (the boathouse or a dock or a woodshed or tool shed) and then fishing the next.[83]

Lloyd Eady built a one-room 16 foot by 24 foot cabin on Whitefish Lake for Mildred and Stanley Welham in 1950. It had a high-peaked green roof and green shutters and was painted regulation white with just a tint of green. Following the latest in architectural design, there were more windows than walls including one at each corner of the cabin and six windows across the front with a door in the middle. As Ruth Welham-Umphrey remembers:

---

[81] Recollections from Rock Lake resident Rose Campbell 2004.

[82] The Halliday Company Ltd, with offices in Hamilton, Ontario and Truro, Nova Scotia sold ready-made kits that included all of the components needed to build a summer cabin. Everything from framing and rafters to paint, nails, windows and roofing were supplied for 2-3 bedroom 20' by 26' buildings.

[83] Recollections from Rock Lake resident Judy Jeffery Hagermann 2004.

"For heat, we had a wood stove (still in use) and for light coal oil lanterns. My mother was afraid of fire and didn't like using the coal oil lanterns, so later the lanterns were replaced with propane lights hanging from the ceiling over the kitchen table. There was no icebox so butter and bottles of milk were kept in the ice-cold creek near the cabin, covered by a wooden shutter."[84]

A few years later the icebox was replaced with a propane fridge when Mildred looked to the creek one day in time to see a bear taking off into the bush with a bottle of milk clasped in its paws. The icebox became a wood box and a three-burner propane stove was placed on top of it. The front windows were lowered so that one could lie in bed and look out across the lake and the cabin was moved back six feet from the water's edge. Moving the cabin was a community affair. All the men of the lake came to help. The cabin was jacked up and placed on rollers. One fellow got underneath to direct the others as they pushed the cabin back. A new outhouse was fashioned with a steel roof, a carpet on the floor and a window (with a screen) in the back wall. It was all wrapped in netting so that no bugs could get in. One friend provided an oak toilet seat. Another carved a wooden door handle and still others made a half moon to place on the front door.[85]

Another building experience of note was at the parcel settled on by Walter and Mary Riddell. Walter had had a very distinguished diplomatic career in the 1930s including being the first deputy minister of Labour in Ontario, Canada's representative at the International Labour Office in Geneva, Switzerland, and Canada's permanent Representative at the League of Nations. In 1937, he went to the Canadian Embassy in Washington DC and in 1940 became the first Canadian High Commissioner in New Zealand. In 1947 while renting a cottage on Lake of Bays, the Riddells came up to Algonquin Park to investigate a retirement home on the advice of a friend, the Honorable Howard Ferguson, a former Premier of Ontario. At the Rock Lake landing, they met Stewart Eady who took them on a tour. Spotting a site up a steep cliff, it took only five minutes for them to make up their minds that this was the spot. On the way back to Lake of Bays, they stopped in at the Park Headquarters at Cache Lake and signed the deed. During the winter of 1948, the builder, a Mr. Patterson of Maple

[84.] Recollections from White Fish Lake resident Ruth Welham-Umphrey 2004.
[85.] Recollections from White Fish Lake resident Ruth Welham Umphrey 2004.

Nook near Huntsville, brought their building materials over the ice by horse. As Mary Eleanor ruefully recollected:

"Mother and Dad tried to place the cottage in a location in order to save every white and red pine on the site. This made it very tricky to take down a dying white pine forty years later. By May the cottage walls and the icehouse were in place. In June the family came up to put in the plumbing and kitchen cupboards. Unfortunately nobody told us about the billions of black flies that immediately attacked, sending several of the Riddells to bed for two days. However by the end of the summer a hand pump, a forty-gallon tank for water, very primitive plumbing and the kitchen cupboards were installed and the cottage had been stained and painted. For the first two years they had an icehouse, but then somebody put the ice in the icehouse in the winter without sawdust between the blocks. When spring came it melted away. Needless to say a Servel Kerosene refrigerator was installed and the icehouse was converted into a sleeping Bunkie. One year, Dad built two crib docks with a raised ramp so that a boat could go through between the swimming island and our part of Third Island. This was a great idea as now the family could go over to the little island and dive into the deep water. Next he devised a cable car from the dock to the cottage that ferried up suitcases and food supplies. Unfortunately as these docks disintegrated and were replace by floating docks the cable car ceased to exist."[86]

Another ambitious building project occurred on Whitefish Lake in the late 1930s. In 1937, the plans to cut a spur from the main road to Whitefish Lake and establish garage accommodation finally came to fruition. Previously in 1935, some of the residents of Rock Lake convened a meeting and wrote to the Department feeling that:

"The road should go to Rock Lake Station not the head of Whitefish as there is an old lumber road that could be pressed into service as it ends within but a short distance of the highway following Rock Creek and wouldn't take much work to make it passable. There are many advantages as the proposed road into Whitefish Lake would mean leaving our cars in the summer and our boats in the winter a long distance from our camps without much supervision whereas bringing

---

[86.] Recollections from Rock Lake resident Mary Eleanor Riddell Morris 2004.

the spur into the head of Rock near the station would mean pretty general protection as there is always someone there."[87]

Unfortunately the Park Superintendent disagreed as a contractor had already been hired to cut out the right of way and clear to Whitefish Lake. 'The DLF was not likely to consider a new spur and build five miles of extra road and two bridges.'[88] He did however agree to allow Ranger McCormick to check out the old lumber road to Rock Lake. McCormick did so in the spring of 1936, drew a small map of the route and wrote a detailed description of the conditions of the land that would have to be crossed. Though no action was taken at that time to extend the road to Rock Lake, the new access road did create an additional new role for Billy Baulke. Using a large 20-foot flat bottom punt (obtained from the Ebinger's after David Ebinger Jr.'s death) that became known as Baulke's pointer, he would transport goods and people to their leaseholds.

With Whitefish Lake now more easily accessible, Charles Young, a professor at Cornell University, expressed interest in 1938 in securing a lease covering a five-acre parcel at the north end of the lake. His intent was to build a central hall and individual cabins and operate a general tourist business similar to Bartlett (Bartlett Lodge), Moore (Killarney Lodge) and Musclow (Musclow Lodge). In addition to renting over-night cabins, Young wanted to rent canoes and sell supplies. He engaged Norman Crewson (the former caretaker from Camp of the Red Gods on Teepee Lake) to both build a house for himself on this property and generally look after Mr. Young's interest.[89] For some unknown reason, the DLF Deputy Minister Cain was concerned and advised Park Superintendent MacDougall:

> *"I would very much appreciate your careful consideration as to the advisability of permitting a camp of this nature to be established. It may be perfectly satisfactory but the season these cabins will be occupied will undoubtedly be considerably longer than the average boys or girls camp and if they are to be only overnight guests, the occupants will be in a considerably different class than those occupying cabins or tents under a supervised tourist camp where the management of the camp is responsible for the decorum and the names of the occupants may be obtained at any time".*[90]

---

[87]. McCourt lease correspondence 1936, Algonquin Park Museum Archives.
[88]. McCourt lease correspondence 1936, Algonquin Park Museum Archives.
[89]. Whitefish Lodge lease correspondence 1938, Algonquin Park Museum Archives.
[90]. Whitefish Lodge lease correspondence 1938, Algonquin Park Museum Archives.

79

Frank McDougall, the Park Superintendent, reassured him that:

> *"The trend of the tourist business seems to be to this type of lodge and while as you say it will cater to a different type of transient business, the transients will be coming through the Park anyway and while they are at a tourist camp they are under better supervision than if such a camp is not available. We have had no trouble with the other camps of similar nature and the experience has been that many who come to stay overnight often prolong their stay if the surroundings are nice. I believe the development will be in the interest of the Department and it will provide at the head of Whitefish Lake a location where boats may be rented and people accommodated. There will be a man Crewson in charge of the place on whom responsibility can be placed and our rangers are in that vicinity to check when necessary."*[1]

Unfortunately, Young's timing was terrible. Soon after the lodge was built, WWII broke out and the tourist business in Ontario dropped off dramatically. By 1943, Young advised the Park Superintendent that he was not at all satisfied and felt that Crewson was failing to live up to the terms of the 10-year contract that the two had put together. He didn't open the lodge for the 1944 season and in 1945 sold the lodge and its buildings to John T. Connolly of Buffalo, New York. Connolly originally intended to fix it up for private use but changed his mind and in 1946 opened Whitefish Lodge again for business. During Connolly's first season of operation, there were major complaints sent to the DLF, against the lodge and again in 1947, to which there was little that the DLF could do. Their detailed inspection indicated that some of the complaints may well have been vindictive but it did give the lodge a somewhat negative reputation. However, business must have been satisfactory, as in 1950 Connolly requested additional land parcels upon which he erected a garage and recreation hall.[92]

[91.] Department of Lands and Forests correspondence 1938, Algonquin Park Museum Archives.

[92.] In 1950 Connolly expressed interest in 'exchanging' his property for some he had found at Lobster Lake in Airy township outside of Algonquin Park. The Department refused this offer and so Connolly kept Whitefish Lodge until his death in 1965 when it was acquired by the crown from his estate and dismantled.

Steve and Judy Jeffrey relaxing on the steps of their new cottage c 1950

Riddell Family sitting on Walter's latest construction project c 1950s

Walter testing a new clothesline that ran from the dock to the cottage c 1950s

The Post War Boom Years

When WWII started in 1939, the three oldest Eady sons joined the Armed Forces. Lloyd and Charlie joined the Army and spent time in England, North Africa, Sicily, Italy, Holland, France, and Germany. The other brother, Eldon, joined the Navy, and made many trips back and forth across the Atlantic during the war on a corvette. However Rock Lake was in the boys' blood. Once he'd returned, Lloyd Eady took a lease on the Madawaska River in 1948 and with his brother Art built a cabin on the site. In 1951, he decided to go to Belgium, and assigned his half interest in his lease to his brother Art.

In the early 1940s the Barclays were still able to come by train from Seneville, Quebec. When the trains finally stopped running to Rock Lake around 1945, Gregor arranged the use of the railway right-of-way from Whitney to Men-Wah-Tay Station. In Whitney, they would be met by George Pearson, the caretaker with his Sylvester one cylinder orange motorcar and a light trailer, who would take them up the private siding. This was certainly a let down from the hey days of arriving on the 'Opeongo'. Later after the rails were lifted they would arrive by car from Whitney.

In 1940, Stewart and Beulah Eady bought the old Rock Lake double section house. With its lathe and plaster walls, the section house soon became the center of the Rock Lake community. Cottagers would also gather there for the weekly arrival of the meat wagon from Whitney. Beulah loved music and would organize dances at the Barclay boathouse that were held every Wednesday and Saturday evening during the summers. She would hire bands and fiddle players from Whitney and would sometimes do the square dance calling herself. These dances were great fun and attended by all of the local residents. Sometimes there were also weekly square dances at Cache Lake. Many of the lake's younger set would attend. Mary Eleanor Riddell recalls one dance where she and Marigold Merritt came home in the early hours of the morning and there was a thick mist on the lake. As she recalled in 2004:

> *"Marigold was very concerned that we might hit the Russell's swimming raft and made me steer out into the lake. After an eternity I asked her to use the flashlight to see how deep the water was – we were nearly at the beach on the other side of the lake. So we started to go back to the west side and lo and behold we nearly hit the swimming dock again. This time we kept very close to shore and probably woke up all the cottages on that side of the lake."*[93]

Also in 1940, McCourt approached the DLF to ask if he could re-open a store at Rock Lake. His idea was to handle a full line of groceries and fresh meats that would cater to the growing cottage community. According to McCourt:

> *"The little store at Whitefish Lake carries only a very small stock of candies, cereals, canned goods and soft drinks and that Baulke's store does not carry any larger stock. [This means that] it is necessary for tourists now to send to Whitney or elsewhere for fresh meats"*[94]

Unfortunately the Park Superintendent disagreed. His view was that there were now enough stores in the area to handle both resident and local tourist trade.

> *"Neither of the two existing stores are turning down any business and if there was any fresh meat business worth going after both Baulke and Crewson would have offered it before now. Most Rock Lake people prefer to have their fresh meat come in from the Highland Inn or Whitney rather than accept the small local choice. The experience of storekeepers in the Park is that there is not enough volume of trade in meats for a storekeeper to keep a stock that would appeal to the tourist trade. The exception is the Highland Inn and even in this case many people prefer to have their meats sent from Huntsville."*[95]

[93.] Recollections from Rock Lake resident Mary Eleanor Riddell Morris 2004.
[94.] McCourt lease correspondence 1940, Algonquin Park Museum Archives.
[95.] McCourt lease correspondence 1940, Algonquin Park Museum Archives.

The war also brought some unexpected excitement to the lake. As Art Eady shared:

> *"In the winter of 1944 we were cutting ice on Rock Lake to store and use in the summer. It was snowing and blowing, and a bit of miserable weather. All at once we heard a small plane circling the lake. The pilot landed close to us with the plane's wheels in the snow, which was about six inches deep. It was a military training plane on its way from Ottawa to Gravenhurst with little or no gas left. The Norwegian pilot had been forced to make an emergency landing. He could speak only broken English and asked if he was in Canada or the USA. We told him that he was still in Canada, about 60 miles from his destination. My father asked me to take the pilot to our house so that he could use the phone and be given something to eat by my mother Beulah. The pilot phoned the airport at Gravenhurst and as it was getting dark by this time; he was told that they would pick him up in the morning. He stayed with us that night. In the morning, they flew in with gas and a pair of skis to strap onto his plane's wheels so that it could take off."*[96]

Park rangers had a rugged life and sometimes had dangerous encounters, but they were a happy bunch and got along well together. Stewart Eady was a dedicated, well-respected park ranger and did his best to 'do the right' thing for the park. But that was not always an easy thing to accomplish. The Park Superintendent Frank MacDougall had believed in the 1930s that logging, recreation, and nature conservation could coexist. Scenic preservation would be given priority over timber extraction as the first principle of 'multiple use' of Algonquin Park. To give his ideas some teeth, he initiated a number of policy initiatives that changed the face of the park significantly. These included insisting that:

- No timber was to be cut within 300 ft of any lake or highway or within 150 feet of any river or portage.
- The interior of the Park should be maintained for all time in a 'state of wilderness' with no public roads, no cottage or lodge development.
- Leaseholders would be restricted to lakes near railway lines or a highway.[97]

---

[96] Recollections from Rock Lake resident Art Eady 2004.

[97] *Protected Places*, by Gerald Killan pg. 61.

He also placed more emphasis on exploiting the Park's revenue generating recreational potential. He added foresters and biologists to the park staff to build a body of scientific research including an annual creel census, studying the role of wolves in the ecosystem, and a fish management program to manage potential over-fishing. At about this same time MacDougall also got interested in conservation issues, likely through his friendship with J. R. Dymond, a zoologist from the Royal Ontario Museum and a Smoke Lake leaseholder. Dymond had helped found the Federation Of Ontario Naturalists in 1934. Their first publication, called 'Sanctuaries and the Preservation of Wildlife in Ontario' was very popular at the time. From Dymond, MacDougall and staff likely learned that wolves were useful in reducing and dispersing deer populations and played an important part in the lake ecology as partially eaten carcasses of their 'kills' provided winter food for small mammals and birds. This knowledge led eventually to the abandonment, though not until well into the 1960s, of the long-standing Park wolf extermination policy[98].

However, day-to-day, the Park Rangers had to manage the complex and sometimes tenuous relationships between loggers and recreationists. Though logging camps were no longer present in the Rock/Whitefish area, McRae Lumber Company had built a sawmill on Lake of Two Rivers into which flowed the Madawaska River. The most troublesome issue for leaseholders with loggers was their perceived indifference to the impact of changing water levels on cottage property. Rock and Whitefish Lake residents would often find in the spring that their property had been substantially damaged by excessively high water that was being used to manage the spring log drives down the Madawaska River. In the spring of 1940, for example, William Pretty came to his cottage only to discover 'that his diving board had been entirely swept away and several logs of the protective breakwater were wrenched out of place.'[99] As he wrote that year:

> *"I am positive that the break up of the ice did not cause this for it was for this purpose that the break-water was built and has withstood the annual break up for the last six or seven years. I wonder if McRae's lumber Company have driven logs through the area and caused the damage."*[100]

[98] *Scientia Canadensis*, Volume 22-23 #51 1998/99, J. R. Dymond and Frank A. MacDougall: Science and Government Policy in Algonquin Provincial Park 1931-1954 by Gerald Killan and George Warecki.

[99] Pretty lease correspondence 1940, Algonquin Park Museum Archives.

[100] Pretty lease correspondence 1940, Algonquin Park Museum Archives.

The McRaes' also had a bad habit of allowing their pigs, which were to be used for food in the winter, to run wild in the woods, which caused many a leaseholder to find their root cellars in ruins.

> *"I am writing to make a complaint to you concerning the nuisance to which we were subjected at Indian Clearing on Rock Lake last summer, and which was continuing to disturb us and threaten damage to our property when the boys came away the middle of September. I refer to the drove of pigs, large and small about 20 in number, running at large through the woods, belonging as we have been told to McRae of Airy. These pigs were an infernal nuisance to us while we were in camp, and stayed in our neighbourhood in spite of our best efforts to drive them off. With their rooting they can tear up a yard and leave it looking like a battlefield of Flanders. We have a root-house we constructed with vast labor and pains, and this is likely to be torn down in ruins by these confounded pigs while we are away. If Mr. McRae wants to keep pigs, let him keep them in a pen and not in our clearing. Will you kindly let me know what relief and protection it lies in your power to give us under these circumstances."[101]*

The Park Ranger and sometimes the Park Superintendent would have to find amicable solutions that kept both parties happy. In resolving the escaping pig problem, late that fall Tom McCormick, the Chief Ranger, reported that 'about the middle of September, McRae shipped out all pigs that were running at large in the section between Rock and Whitefish Lakes. Since then we have not noticed any along the track or around the cottages.'[102]

As well documented by Gerald Killan in his book on the history of Ontario's Park system, after WWII, 'pressures due to rapid population growth, urbanization, a rising standard of living, increased leisure time, more personal mobility and an improved highway network, produced an explosion in outdoor recreation demand and quickly strained existing parklands beyond acceptable limits'. Campgrounds, children's camps, and resorts were filled to capacity in the summer. The main public campground at Lake of Two Rivers campground was suffering from overuse and the once pristine water in Cache Lake was polluted and unfit for drinking. In 1950, over 1,000 floatplanes flew 1,137 anglers to isolated parts of the park interior. The number of cars entering Algonquin Park grew from 28,662

---

[101]. Zorbaugh lease correspondence 1931, Algonquin Park Museum Archives.
[102]. Zorbaugh lease correspondence 1931, Algonquin Park Museum Archives.

in 1950 to 47,200 in 1953. The number of cottage leases doubled from 1950 to 1954 including 22 new additions to the Rock/Whitefish area. J. R. Dymond wrote 'about the litter problem that was spreading throughout the park and the damage that was being inflicted upon natural features by recreationists insensitive to the environment and lacking basic woodcraft skills. The resulting garbage dumps (required to service these new users) attracted dozens of foraging bears that began to terrorize cottagers and damage property. By October 1953 over 100 animals had to be shot by the rangers with the resulting publicity damaging the parks reputation as the province's leading game reserve.'[103]

The Park Ranger's job reverted from one of catching poachers to nearly becoming one. Bear incidents were frequent and very frightening for those involved. One summer, Mary Eleanor Riddell Morris was visited nightly by a three-legged bear that would walk by her screened in sleeping porch. Stewart Eady finally had to shoot it, as it was making the rounds of cottages and campsites all over the lake. On another occasion, her son Rob Morris, then 15, decided take a fish he'd caught to a young couple camping on the nearby campsite. As he paddled up he found the couple enjoying their dinner admiring the sunset, totally unaware that just behind was a huge bear standing on his back paws. Rob, with his heart in his mouth, told them to move slowly to their canoe and not to pick up anything. All three retreated to one of the cottages on the Island. The poor couple, were in such a state of shock that they couldn't speak. Later in the week the bear was seen crashing through the dense bush on the other side of the bay and was shot near Whitney soon after. In another bear incident, a leaseholder was trapped in their cottage by a rogue bear that had already been tagged three times. DLF hunters tried unsuccessfully to entice the bear away with ripe food from Killarney Lodge.[104] As commented by Don Pepler in 1946:

"I just wanted to repeat what I told you that I am 100% satisfied with the treatment you people give all of us in the Park; looking after our welfare like one big family. I would also like to say that your representative at Rock Lake Stewart Eady has been and is a very efficient member of your administration, and is extremely kind to all of us in all sorts of our various problems."[105]

[103.] *Protected Places*, by Gerald Killan, pgs 76-78
[104.] Recollections from Rock Lake resident Mary Eleanor Riddell Morris 2004.
[105.] Pepler lease correspondence 1946, Algonquin Park Museum Archives.

But bears weren't the only animals that could cause trouble. One year Brad Steinberg and a friend snowshoed down the plowed Rock Lake Road in to the cottage for an early start to the season. They had a golden retriever Timber, with them, and a toboggan with supplies for the trip. The boys saw a large bull moose in the woods. As they continued down our driveway, they were charged by the moose. Brad and friend dove into the bushes, but Timber was badly trampled. Brad managed to stuff his scarf and glove into the gaping wound in her chest and carry the dog back out to the vehicle and on to a vet. Timber had surgery, a bad infection and a lengthy recovery, but her ribs were wired back together. Luckily the moose's hooves had missed her vital organs.[106]

Another set of fascinating wild life experiences happened at the Miller lease on Galeairy Lake. Galeairy Lake, just a short portage away, was a popular fishing and picnicking destination for the Rock Lake community. In the early years it was known as Long Lake and was one of those lakes that spanned the boundary of Algonquin Park with the town of Whitney at the far east end. Squaw Point located diagonally opposite Loon Island in the channel heading towards the Narrows contained the only leased parcel on the lake, a sharp contrast to the many parcels leased on Rock Lake. According to son Robert Miller:

> "The Algonquin Park portion of Galeairy Lake has never known extensive active leases. My father, Rev. Roy Miller, a Presbyterian pastor from Pennsylvania was first made aware of Algonquin Park by two fellow Presbyterian pastors Rev. E. C. Good and Rev. W. Byers. Both with their respective wives were lovers of the outdoors and had camped in the area since 1928 and taken a lease with high school teacher Jim Knoh and Dr. John Walsh in 1933. With age, tenting became more difficult, so in 1946 my father obtained a lease and had built a simple three room cottage that we named Squaw Point. According to some local old timers at the time, it was a point where nomadic Algonquin Indians would leave their squaws before going to a trading post located across the lake in Francois Bay (now Purcell Cove)."[107]

[106.] Recollections from Rock Lake resident Helen Steinberg 2004.
[107.] Recollections from Galeairy Lake resident Robert Miller 2003.

There was one other leaseholder on the lake; Oliver Post who had settled in 1920 for a parcel on one of the islands, and two illegal cabins, one in Farm Bay and the other on Fogey's or Brown's Point. Later a children's camp was established in 1950 in Forest Bay at the foot of the portage to Prottler Lake. Run by two returning Canadian servicemen from Toronto, Robert Telford and James Alexander McKenchnie, it only survived a couple of years and was forced to close when one of their campers came down with polio."[108] The DLF acquired the property in 1954 but the buildings weren't removed until 1966. Contrary to regulations, the Pennsylvania collective headed by Dr. Welsh built a number of cottages on their single lease using components from buildings found at an abandoned logging camp in what is now Purcell Cove. According to Robert Miller:

> *"Byers and Goods dismantled the buildings and floated them across the lake, log by log, where they were reassembled and used until after WWII at which time they were replaced with cottages built with conventional lumber. We would frequently get together with them on Sundays to share a potluck dinner, which largely featured bass and trout. My mother's specialty was baked lake trout with bread stuffing, which was delicious. These frequent Sunday 'pot luck' meals and the accompanying fellowship were enjoyed by all."[109]*

Meanwhile Rev. Miller with his wife Florence continued to come to Algonquin Park every year and always enjoyed Algonquin Park to the fullest. As their son Robert recalled in 2003:

> *"Nothing [could] compare to the action experienced in playing a small mouth bass nor the subsequent mouth-watering meal. Of course, the big bass caught now are more apt to be 3-4 pounds rather than the 6-7 pounds of earlier years. A mounted 7-pound plus small mouth bass caught by my father graced our home for years. Likewise, my mother was a skilled fisherwoman and the Park booklet "Fishing in Algonquin*

[108.] Recollections from Galeairy Lake resident Robert Miller 2003.

[109.] According to the Welsh lease records, in 1954 this was one of the first leases to be issued without a renewability clause, in 1975 it was one of the first to expire under the 1954 Park Policy With the support of the Algonquin Park Residents Association (APRA) the family along with several others from Canoe Lake appealed to the Ombudsman's office but their appeal was denied. Not long after the Crown, due to political pressure at Queen's Park, had a change of heart and agreed to renew the lease along with two others on Canoe Lake that were in this same situation. But by then it was too late, the Good and Byers families had resettled outside of the Park. The Welshs disappeared from the scene completely.

Provincial Park still shows an un-named photo of her holding an eel she caught in Galeaiy Lake in the early 1930s."[110]

Another remarkable wildlife story involved a Canadian Ruffed Grouse.

"Upon arriving in early August to open up the cottage, I came around one corner and a Ruffed Grouse with two peeps met me head on. The grouse immediately was protective of the peeps, swelling up like a balloon as she confronted me. A simple "coo-coo" voiced by me convinced her that she had nothing to fear, for she immediately deflated and we were on a friendly basis for the rest of the summer. There was nothing tentative about my acceptance, for mother grouse would bring the peeps by every 2-3 days. On one occasion while we were having a cookout in front of the cottage, mother grouse dusted herself on the path while the peeps were busy picking and eating from shrubs and bushes here and there. Most remarkable was the bond established with me. On hearing their faint sounds, even in the distant wood, I would 'coo' and immediately hear the distinctive sound of beating grouse wings and mother grouse flew in to greet me. My closest encounter was experienced at our outhouse. I "cooed' and in she flew, landing on the peak of 'biffy' and then came down to the edge of the roof where, literally, eyeball to eyeball, we briefly 'cooed' to each other before she flew back to the peeps. We never attempted to touch nor did we ever feed the grouse."[111]

Yet another amazing experience took place in the water just off the Miller dock.

"With my profession as a sailor and submariner, I had developed a great love of the sea and all that is within it. Galeaiy became the benefactor of this love, and I still am often seen with my mask, snorkel and fins swimming the lake to discover its underwater delights. Fish in Galeaiy normally move quickly away when confronted. They are curious about human swimmers, but observe from a distance that often precludes me from seeing them in the limited visibility water. This norm was changed one summer when, much to my amazement, I came upon a snapping turtle and a bass swimming together, there normally not being any harmony between the two. (How many fishermen have

[110.] Recollections from Galeaiy Lake resident Robert Miller 2003.
[111.] Recollections from Galeaiy Lake resident Robert Miller 2003.

pulled up their stringers to find only fish heads left after a turtle feasted on the rest). I examined the big turtle about 25 pounds while the bass watched from a position close-by. Upon concluding, I swam away and the 1 1/2, pound bass followed, thus the beginning of another summer friendship.

I swim most days whether the weather is hot, cold, calm or stormy. My bass friend, although not waiting at the water's edge most often would join up with me as the daily swim progressed and followed me very closely whether I was diving to investigate the bottom or swimming on the surface. I would occasionally put on a burst of speed with my fins, which would cause the bass to race past me until I slowed at which point the bass would come back, look in my face mask, as to say; ""You can't beat me! Why Try" When I would stop and rest with my feet on the bottom, the bass took up position between the calves of my legs and wouldn't move until I was ready to swim again. Friend bass was not above harmlessly nipping me on the body, it not being clear whether it wanted to get on with the swim or whether there was indecision as to my tastiness and edibility. I started to carry a few kernels of dried corn, which it would eat out of my hand. My final day of vacation, I swam one last time with the bass. It was not there the following summer. Not having had this experience repeated over the years, I am not sure whether this bass was 'crazy' or perhaps 'extra smart'. I like to think it was the later which made our time together so very special."[112]

Miller Family get together on Galeairy Lake c 1934

112. Memories from Galeairy Lake resident Robert Miller 2003

Miller Homestead at Squaw Point on Galeairy Lake c 1934

Whitefish Lodge c 1957 APMA#5407

Using a docked airplane as a sunbathing spot c 1940s

Willard Taylor in his 3/4 hsp ELTO c 1940s

Willard Taylor (L) driving his Fleetwin racing motor c 1940s

Howard Jeffery and Robert Taylor with lake trout c 1950s

Successful fishing with Dr. Wilson (C), Keith Russell (L), and Anne Johnson (R)

Rock Lake community get together (date unknown)

Billy and Gertrude Baulke in later years c 1950

Park Superintendent Jim Taylor (L), William Greer (R) Park Plane 1940 at Greer's Dock

Newly built Greer cabin 1942

Dr. Watson (L) and Billy Baulke (R) 1943

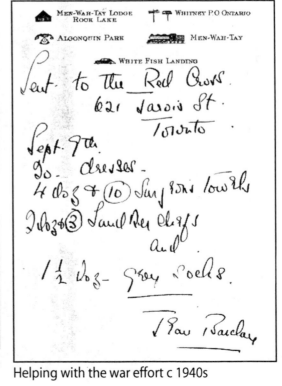

Helping with the war effort c 1940s

Taylor had great plans for the Rock Lake property. His idea was to lease some land from the CNR near Baulke's Point on the north end of what is now the Rock Lake Campsite No. 2. He then bought the Rock Lake Station double house that the Eady's had vacated and planned to move it to his site and convert it to a summer cottage. Unfortunately, he fell from a scaffold in 1950 while building his dream home in Port Credit, and died in 1952.[119]

With increased use of the Park, there also came an increase in the number of accidents on or about the lake, and the residents became quite good at water rescue. One year a floatplane took off from nearby Pen Lake and lost a propeller. The plane crashed into the lake and rolled over, but the three passengers made it to shore by floating on cushions.[120] Another year, on the May 24th weekend, leaseholders Joan and Lorne Somers pulled 3 people out of the lake who had dumped in their canoe. Unfortunately, one died of hypothermia, but the Somers were presented with an OPP Commissioner Citation for their efforts.[121] Alas, not always were leaseholders or the Park Ranger able to get there in time. In one case, a canoe with army cadets capsized when it got too close to a forestry plane that was taking off. One of the boys, unable to swim and not wearing a life jacket, instantly sank to the bottom of the lake.[122]

Another May 24th Weekend incident involved Duncan MacGregor, the father of writer and Globe and Mail columnist Roy MacGregor. The Beatons were outside working around the cabin when Helen looked onto the lake and saw this man in the water with his right arm slung over the side of the boat. Jack and son John dashed out in their boat to rescue him but they just couldn't pull him out of the water. He had on a long down jacket and lumberjack boots. The water was frigid and he was so cold that he couldn't call for help. They pulled him alongside the boat to the shore and with one on each side of him literally dragged him up to the cottage. He was trying to get his feet under himself, but just couldn't do it. Jack got him into dry clothes, gave him a shot of whisky, heated up some soup and later delivered him back to the lumber camp all in one piece.

[119.] Recollections from Rock Lake resident Robert Taylor 2003 & 2004.
[120.] Recollections from Rock Lake resident Art Eady 2004.
[121.] Recollections from Rock Lake resident Helen Beaton, 2004.
[122.] Recollections from Rock Lake resident Art Eady 2004.

Another incident involved a young Brad Steinberg and a friend. They had decided to go cross-country skiing along the Booth Rock Trail. Foolishly they started out late in the day and, when dusk started to fall, they decided to take a short cut back to the cottage. Alas, they became disoriented, but luckily had a few matches as well as a few survival skills and managed to build a fire. They made a bed of sorts under the roots of an upturned tree and spent a long cold night huddled around the meager fire. In the morning, they made it back to the cottage and eventually thawed out. Aside from a little frostbite, both survived the ordeal unscathed and, hopefully wiser.[123]

There was also a growing sense of community as people got together to help each other out and deep friendships were forged. As Helen Steinberg remembers so fondly:

> "Our neighbours, Bill and Hazel Bishop were originally from Newfoundland, and had a perfect little cabin down the river from us. Bill told us that he had camped in the Park for years before they bought their lease. We soon discovered that Bill was an avid trout fisherman and so began a friendship that was strong and unchanging throughout Bill's life. He and my husband Brian fished together nearly every day for many years, and Hazel became a surrogate grandmother for our son Brad. She made him his own batch of chocolate chip cookies each time she came up to the cottage. When any of the kids caught a fish or had an adventure, they would run down the lane to tell the Bishops their story. Bill was charming, with a quick, rich wit and a Newfie's earthy wisdom and sense of humour. He introduced us to Rock lake lore, and taught us the famous toast, "Long may your big jib draw"! After Hazel died, Bill joined us for most evening meals during the summer, and enjoyed telling me that he had a "cast-iron stomach [and therefore was willing to try just about anything]."[124]

123. Recollections from Rock Lake resident Helen Steinberg 2004.
124. Recollections from Rock Lake resident Helen Steinberg 2004.

The 1954 Change of Heart

Though leaseholders played only a small and quite insignificant part, the end result of the problems of overcrowding, rowdyism, the deterioration of the natural environment and political pressure from conservationists, was a new Park policy that was introduced in 1954. It's objective was to 'restore Algonquin Park to a more natural state'.[125] Frank MacDougall, now the Deputy Minister of Lands and Forests, who had been a friend to many of the leaseholders, issued Lands and Recreational Areas Circular No. 24 to all division chiefs and field offices that would change the attitudes of leaseholders forever. With no public hearings, nor public consultation of any sort, a new government policy on the management of leaseholds in Algonquin Park was confirmed to over 100 people at the Canoe Lake and District Leaseholders Association annual meeting on Sunday August 1, 1954. Leaseholders were informed that:

- Existing leases could stay but no new leases, 'licenses of occupation' or permits would be granted for private, public or commercial purposes.
- Existing leases could be renewed, but would not contain any provision for further renewal.
- The assignment of existing leases to husband, wife or children was allowed, but the Crown reserved the right to acquire the lease if the desire was to sell or transfer to any other person.
- The Department would now require pre-approval of all plans before any

---

[125.] Canoe Lake and District Leaseholder Association Minutes 1954.

building or clearing of land so as to not have any unnecessary addition to asset value of buildings, etc.

- No leasee would be permitted to encroach on land beyond the limits of the land covered by their lease.

- The Department would now enforce the regulations prohibiting the leaving of boats by non-residents on certain lakes for fishing etc. and would soon put in place restrictions of airplanes on and over the Park except for Department inspection and fire control.

- Lease properties could be sold as long as the Department was given the first right of refusal. If the Department didn't want the property then it could be sold to another buyer but the buyer would need to accept the existing terms of the lease.

The Algonquin Park resident community was in shock. After over 40 years of encouragement and support, leaseholders of any sort, including those who had started children's camps, commercial lodges, built cabins, were now considered unacceptable. One of the reasons given for the change in thinking was to respond to huge pressure that the Department was getting at the time to grant leases for all kinds of commercial uses. The view was that these uses would destroy the primary purposes of the Park as a public recreational area, wildlife reserve and natural forest. There was a movement afoot to try to recapture the natural character of the provincial parks.

For the first few years, residents could hardly believe it let alone understand the motives behind it. For them the problems in the Park were as a result of unregulated logging and the irresponsibility of transient car campers, not residents whose hearts and souls were imbedded in each cabin log and vested in every living thing in their surroundings. But for some, more heartbreak was yet to come.

Included in the policy was an intent to 'buy back' any existing private 'patented' land that was in the Park and as many leaseholds as possible. Not surprisingly, the first target was the Barclay Estate. Ian Barclay, after having attended McGill as an undergraduate and Harvard to study labour law had settled in Vancouver where he later became president of British Columbia Forest Products.[126] Joan, (who also did undergraduate work at

---

[126.] Ian retired from BCFP but still runs his own company at the ripe old age of 83. He had one daughter Deborah who married a prominent doctor (Dr. David Rollins) and lives in the Vancouver area.

McGill and then studied archeology at Ottawa University) was in Montreal. She had married John Drummond in 1946 and had a daughter Robin born in 1952 and son Timothy born in 1953.[127] Both were finding the upkeep of the estate more and more difficult and expensive. The pressure from Frank MacDougall, who had at one point been a dear family friend, was relentless. There were suggestions that if sold to DLF the Estate might become a luxury resort and even other rumours that it would be converted to a senior's retirement residence or leased to a non-profit organization for health or recreational purposes.

Eventually, an agreement was made, and in 1955 the approximately 700 acres complete with all buildings, including the boathouse at Gordon Lake, became the property of the Crown. The summer of 1955 was the last summer that the Barclays were in residence at Rock Lake. According to lease record correspondence, it turned out that realistically; preserving the property was not in the cards as the Fire Marshall's office wasn't supportive of any of the new ideas.[128] The end came later that year when the DLF burned down all of the buildings leaving only some of the foundations. As Helen Beaton, a Rock Lake resident who had arrived in 1950, remembers:

> "[We heard that] the beautiful Barclay summer residence with triple boat house/recreation room with its gorgeous huge fireplace all now emptied [was] slated to be burned that coming winter. [We] found an open window crawled through and took a look inside. It was such a crime to burn the beautiful wood in the walls, the staircase, and the floor. We saw one small lonely footstool, which had been left behind; saved it from the torch, and have it still. After it was all over, some of the boathouse fireplace stones lying in the water were lovingly collected and safely embedded in our fireplace. Built by Jack Beaton and numerous friends over several years, the mantle is solid oak into which he wrote the words 'God rest you all who linger here' in English script and a friend Edgar Burke carved it. Mr. Burke Sr. (Alec) was an amateur taxidermist and gave us a deer head, which hangs on the upper part of the fireplace. Also cemented in was a stone brought back from Banff where we went on our honeymoon, rocks for Helen's parents

---

[127] John's family was related to the Birks jewelry family of Montreal and had Drummond St. in Montreal named after them. Robin died of Lupus in 1995 and son Timothy who is married to Joanne lives in Ottawa.

[128] Camp Douglas lease correspondence 1955, Algonquin Park Museum Archives.

(Elizabeth and Alexander Kovach) and footprints for each of our two children John and Kathryn at the ages of 3 and 4 months respectively just above the mantle on either side of the fireplace.[129]

So ended the Booth-Fleck-Barclay-Drummond experience on Rock Lake. As Joan Drummond said in 2004 with tears in her eyes:

"So many marvelous memories. Amos the Indian teaching me how to paddle the birch bark canoe, walking on the gunnels, tipping it, righting it, and getting on board again. Learning of the edible plants and roots in the woods, the moss on the trees, telling you which way was north, the marvelous bass fishing in Gordon Lake. I became an expert frog catcher, and 'dew wormer', never cringing about baiting and releasing fish, much to my brother's delight who would not touch either. (Shades of my grandmother!) It was from Billie that I learnt that a good spit on the bait always caught more fish too! I often took my small pup tent and went off on my explorations, down to the end of the lake by the huge rock cliff, or half way to Gordon Lake, where I discovered some Indian caves and drawings. Sitting on top of Booth Rock for hours waiting until the cloud formation was just right to take pictures with my Brownie box camera. The great baseball games we played at the Rock Lake Station beach and field area where we used cow dung as bases. The Sunday services at the Baulke house where we really 'rocked and rolled' under the tutelage of Louise Baulke, the deaconess, who played on the old pump and roller organ. But above all I remember the magnificent northern lights, the majesty of the huge pine trees, the blue of the lake, the haunting call of the loons and the mournful cry of the wolves. I still to this day get tears in my eyes when I remember my beloved Rock Lake, the nearest place to heaven that I will ever be"[130]

Also in 1955, Billy Baulke died and like the Barclay Estate, soon after, his cottages were acquired by DLF and destroyed. The site was cleared and became, as previously mentioned, Rock Lake Public Campsite No. 2. In 1964, when the CNR returned the right-of-way for the Rock Lake area to the DLF they canceled the station house License of Occupation that the Eady's held, and the building was also razed by fire. By then, Stewart Eady had long retired to Killaloe. On the site, right outside the McCourt's front

---

[129.] Recollections from Rock Lake resident Helen Beaton 2003.
[130.] Recollections from former Rock Lake resident Joan Barclay Drummond 2004.

door, was built the first Algonquin Park amphitheater on the ground sloping down to Rock Creek. A 110-volt propane generator was installed to feed the campsite. It ran from morning until 10 p.m. to supply electricity to the office and the nearby washrooms. Though the noise eventually became 'white noise' the real problem was the dust generated by all of the cars coming to the shows two times a week.[131] Eventually it was moved to Lake of Two Rivers for easier access from Highway 60 and on the power gride, which then made slide shows possible.

Unfortunately, like the Baulkes, the building of a public campground across the creek (at Rock Lake) created many problems for James Stringer, who worked for the Ontario Provincial Police and had taken over in 1945 the Johnson lease where the river meets Rock Creek.

As recounted by Stringer in 1959,

> *"In the late 40s I went off, on several occasions leaving my tools completely exposed so that anyone could pick them up, returning only to find everything as I had left it. Certainly it has been an area free from break-ins and vandalism through the past years. However now people [camping at the Rock Lake Campsite] come from the parking area and take my boats without permission. On more than one occasion Ranger Eady has made people return our boats under the above-mentioned circumstances. On another occasion six people walked in my yard without permission, while we were at the cottage, turned my canoe over, and had their pictures taken sitting in the canoe while it rested on sticks and roots on the ground."[132]*

Eventually Stringer decided that the best thing to do was to sell the property back to the DLF. It took two years to negotiate an agreement. When concluded, Stringer was under the impression that the price did not include the existing contents of the cabins and the storehouse. As he said:

> *'We continued our insurance policy covering the items with the understanding that it would be safe until they (the DLF) had occasion to use it and at such time I would be informed and given ample time to remove the furnishings.[133]"*

[131.] According to Ron Tozer, former Park Naturalist, the theatre programs were held two nights a week each at Rock Lake, Lake of Two Rivers and the Cache Lake Rec. Hall. On the seventh day, the programs were held at the children's camps in the area.

[132.] Stringer lease correspondence 1959, Algonquin Park Museum Archives.

[133.] Stringer lease correspondence 1961, Algonquin Park Museum Archives.

Alas in the winter of 1961, without notifying Stringer, the buildings and most of their contents were burned and destroyed. A limited amount of the furnishings had been removed but all of the rest of Stringers' possessions were gone. Park officials were adamant that anything of value had been removed to a storehouse and refused to negotiate a settlement. Unfortunately, according to Stringer, the items found in the storehouse didn't nearly match his list of valued possessions. How it was resolved in the end is not recorded in the lease records.

In 1961, Ida McCourt died and in her will left the original log building and contents to Oriole, and the Shawna Lodge building and contents to Myrtle and Vernon together. Unfortunately, the park regulations did not enable this type of lease division, so title to the lease was transferred to all three as 'tenants-in-common'. It took until 1964 to sort out the transfer as the DLF was interested in acquiring the property. Oriole was supportive of selling to the Crown but Myrtle and Vernon were not. She approached Premier Bill Davis, whom she knew, and effectively communicated to him the degree to which 'Old Shawna' was the family home. He intervened with Kelso Roberts, the Minister of Lands and Forests, and in 1964 the negotiations were suspended. The lease was renewed without further ado, but backdated to 1963.[134] By then, Oriole and Vernon had retired. None of the cousins had much time to spend in Algonquin Park, so the Taylors became the primary users.

By the 1970s, very little had been accomplished in turning Algonquin Park back to its natural state. In fact, the reality was that logging continued unabated, as did car camping. The resulting overuse of campgrounds and hiking trails along the Highway 60 corridor was causing great damage to the Park. Interior camp routes (especially the Canoe Lake to Burnt Island circuit) had become major thoroughfares and the conditions of the campsites deplorable. Some Rock Lake residents had had enough. One of the most vocal was Crozier Taylor (grandson of Henry James Taylor) who in the 1960s was an executive at Canada Life Assurance Company and went on to own the 'Pillar and Post' restaurant in Niagara-on-the-Lake. He abandoned his lease in 1975 with the view (as he wrote at the time to the Editor of the Globe and Mail newspaper) that:

"This land, once protected and revered by the leaseholders that had

---

[134.] McCourt lease correspondence 1963, Algonquin Park Museum Archives.

the foresight to venture north decades ago is fast becoming a Coney Island. From the turn of the century, my forefathers evolved and grew with the Algonquin experience. As a lad, I learned very quickly to love and respect the simple life of the North. Our parents and forest rangers had taught us how to conduct ourselves in the bush and how to care for the land and wildlife. The 1954 policy was established to turn the park back to nature and at the same time gradually turn out the few cottagers when their leases expired. Consistent with this came a plan to build campsites for transient campers who since have come in droves onto a few southern park lakes. Peaceful little lakes have been turned into urban intersections. Raping the forests, burning, littering and looting have become commonplace. There were 30 fires from recreational sources in 1974 and 67 fires from recreational sources in 1975. The Park is less back to nature now than it was 22 years ago. We haven't seen a deer in years, moose that far south in the park are now practically unheard of and even the birds including the loons are disappearing. … The oil on the lake surface was getting thicker every year —the debris around the shore looking more like Lake Erie. The portages look like long lines of garbage dumps. The animals have fled and the fish have just about given up."[135]

By the early 1980s, when both Vernon and Myrtle died, it had became clear that the McCourt lease, sitting as it did right in the middle of the access way to the Rock Lake Campground, did not fit into the MNR plans for the Rock Lake area. Alas, the 'tenants-in-common' lease arrangement, which seemed like such a good idea at the time, meant that upon Myrtle and Vernon's deaths the full title transferred to Oriole, and no claims by the descendents of Myrtle and Vernon were recognised. Oriole was not willing to deed the lease to Myrtle's son Robert Taylor and for whatever reasons elected not to join the 1979 Plan for common lease end dates. This meant that when the lease expired in 1984, the Taylors would have to leave. They contested Oriole's handling of the lease and continued to use the place for three years past the 1984 termination date by refusing to leave. It was Park policy not to burn down a place with chattels in it and a lock still on the door. After extensive negotiations in 1987, the final official position was that the park officials would consider renewing the lease only if the family

---

[135.] *Toronto Globe and Mail,* Letter to the Editor July 1975 by Crozier Taylor.

paid three years back rent (a calculation based on a @ $10 per foot per year for the original 330 foot of railway right-of-way. This was felt by the family to be unreasonable. Besides, living in the middle of a public campground was not considered an Algonquin Park ideal location. So with a heavy heart the Taylors gave up the lease. In the fall of 1987, they were ordered to remove anything of value and 'Old Shawna Lodge' was burned to the ground. Today all that remains is the Bell Telephone Co. box in Ida's lilac bushes and a few of her roses in what was once her back garden. Other than the long straight road that leads to Rock Lake Campground No. 2 there are no other signs that here once stood a vibrant little community at Rock Lake Station.

However, the Rock Lake/ Whitefish Lake community, though now much smaller, still lives on. It's members number around 35 families and it is incredibly strong and vibrant. They are located on the western shore of Rock Lake, along the Madawaska River and the south end of Whitefish Lake, with a few scattered elsewhere on the lakes. Camp Douglas is gone, as is Whitefish Lodge. The wide-open meadow at the north end of White Fish Lake is used as a group campsite. Residents keep a close eye on this and the antics of Rock Lake Campground visitors, and every year rescue a few from disaster. Their vigilance in protecting the natural environment is legendary. Stewart Eady would be proud that his legacy of care and concern for the Park lives on.

Natasha Taylor on her cabin stoop c 1980s

Special Rock Lake Station Memories

- The year (1949) when Marigold Merritt had a party and served spiked punch. The next morning she found she had the perfect mousetrap as the jugs were filled with mice, who had died happily in the gin drink! (Mary Eleanor Morris)

- Where else but in Algonquin Park can you introduce your children and grandchildren to the beauties of nature, orange and red sunsets, glorious autumn colours, quietness, stillness and a place where they can study birds, see deer, marten beaver, bears, Great Blue Herons and even cow moose swimming over to calve. (Mary Eleanor Morris)

- The year the Park plane brought in serum for whooping cough one summer when the young Pepler children got sick at their grandfather's cottage. (Peggy Sharpe)

- Swimming parties in the afternoon and bonfires with cocoa and singing in the evening were highlights of summer holidays on Rock Lake. Mornings were for chores, of course. Pen Lake rapids or the dam at Galeairy were our favorite picnic sites where the swimming was fun. (Peggy Sharpe)

- Winter trips to the Park were an adventure. We drove to the McRae lumber camp at Lake Of Two Rivers where we had lunch [and tasted some of their] fabulous raisin pie. Then Don McRae sent us by handcar along the tracks to Men-Wah-Tay. George Pearson and his horse transported us from there across the lake. We skied on the hill behind his place. A barrel adapted to a log-burning stove in the middle of the cabin and the wood cook stove kept us warm. A hole in the lake provided water and one year we had a fine ice rink for skating and hockey. Laying on our bunks for cots in the loft at night the logs of the cabin made loud cracking noises. There are spruce logs taken from along the trail to Lake Louise in 1939. Perhaps they were new enough that the sap was still freezing in them. (Peggy Sharpe)

- Grandma and Grandpa Allan believing that the cottage was built on a log slide site because of the large numbers of enormous logs lying around the site, some so large they couldn't be cut so were buried in a trench. How earth from wheelbarrow amounts to what could be spooned into a pail was moved from wherever it could be found to fill in depressions in the paths and how rocks were moved to shore up the bank on the shoreline to prevent further erosion. (Fred Allan)

- Wolves howling on shore at the deer escaping by swimming across the lake. Paddling through the fog and coming upon a pack of wolves and their freshly killed breakfast. Beaver swimming by and otters frolicking at twilight. (Fred Allan)

- The Indians that used to come around the lake in the early 1930's selling baskets and quill boxes. (Maud Merritt)

- Canoeing, swimming, hiking, exploring, fishing, stargazing, reading, playing games, visiting with friends, sliding down Pen Lake rapids, listening to the loons at night; waking up on a chilly morning to a blazing, crackling fire; the smell of coffee, bacon and eggs, bread toasted on the hot coals, sitting out on the dock with a hot drink on a foggy morning, canoeing through the mist, and hiking up Booth Rock for a spectacular view. (Helen Beaton)

- The year we held a Treasure Hunt by canoe for the children all around the lake and the Thanksgiving weekend when a seaplane landed on the lake and cruised up to our dock. He said he was flying to his place in the Muskokas but there was a storm ahead. Our place was the only smoke he spotted in the area. He tied the plane up to their dock, stayed overnight and took off early the next morning after a frigid swim and breakfast. (Helen Beaton)

- The beacon on the dock trick: guide your children home at night with an oil lamp flickering on the dock. (Robert Taylor)
- Watching with guarded amusement the canoe misadventures of visiting campers, people sitting backwards, or facing each other, zigzagging and paddle flipping down the river. (Helen Steinberg)

Bibliography

1. Killan, Gerald, *Protected Places: A History of Ontario's Provincial Parks System* Dundurn Press Ltd in association with the Ontario Ministry of Natural Resources, Toronto 1993.

2. MacKay, Roderick and Reynolds, William, *Algonquin,* Stoddart Publishing Co. Ltd., Toronto1993.

3. Trinnell, John Ross, *J. R. Booth Life and Times of an Ottawa Lumber King*, Tree House Publishing, Ottawa 1998.

4. Saunders, Audrey, *The Algonquin Story*, Ontario Department of Lands and Forests, Toronto, 1946.

5. Killan, Gerald and Warecki, George, J. R. Dymond and Frank A. MacDougall: Science and Government Policy in Algonquin Provincial Park 1931-1954, *Scientia Canadensis*, Volume 22-23 #51 1998/99.

6. Noble, William, *Ontario Archaeological Society*, Publication No. 11, June 1968.

7. *Cache Flash,* a publication of the Cache Lake Leaseholders Association.

8. Written and oral recollections from Rock, Whitefish and Galeairy Lake Residents including Robert Taylor, Joan Barclay Drummond, William Greer, Art Eady, Brian, Brad and Helen Steinberg, Judy Hagerman, Rose Campbell, Mary Eleanor Morris, Peggy Sharpe, Robert Holmes, Leslie and Fred Allan Jr., Helen Beaton, Ruth Welham Umphrey, Mary Fretz and Robert Miller.

9. Lease correspondence and interviews in the AP Museum Archives 1905-1991.

Photo and Graphic Credits:

1. Book layout and chapter designs by Troy Chasey of Capitola Design, Capitola, CA

2. Robert Taylor Collection of family photographs from over 100 years on Rock Lake include:

   Page 10 (Middle and bottom Two), Pages 15 and 16, Pages 18 and 19, Page 21 (bottom), Pages 29 - 31, Pages 39 & 40, Page 45 (Middle), Pages 46 & 47, Page 92 (Bottom Two) and Page 93 (Top Two and Bottom), Page 108

3. William Greer Taylor Collection of Henry Taylor photographs and others collected over the last 60 years from the Baulke, Merritt and Watson families include:

   Page 9, Page 10 (Top Two), Page 17, Page 41, Page 42 & 43, Page 45 (Top Two and Bottom Two), Page 93 (Middle) and Page 94

4. Rock Lake Family Collections

   Page 57 – Eady Family Collection, Page 81 (Top) – Hagerman Family Collection, Page 81 (Middle and Bottom) – Riddell Family Collection, Page 91 – Miller Family Collection, Page 92 (Top) – Miller Family Collection

5. Algonquin Park Museum Archives

   Page 56 – APMA #1268 J. Leech Porter, Page 92 (Middle) APMA #5407 – Ministry of Natural Resources

6. Excerpts

   Page 21 (Top Two) – Canadian Architect and Builder Volume 13 Nov. 1900, Page 73 – The Halliday Company Limited Catalogue – Date Unknown

7. Glin Bennett Collection

   Page 21 (middle), Page 28, Page 67, Page 68

ISBN 1412066263

9 781412 066266